# Santa Fe Woman

## The American West Series

# Laura Stapleton

ISBN: 9781726783491

# DEDICATION

For Donna.

# CONTENTS

# ACKNOWLEDGMENTS

I travel the Santa Fe Trail from Kansas City, Missouri, to Fort Dodge, Kansas at least three times a year. I've also lived and traveled from Amarillo, Texas, to Las Vegas, New Mexico, and down to Albuquerque. Despite my firsthand knowledge, I'd like to thank William E. Hill for his book, *The Santa Fe Trail, Yesterday and Today*. His work helped fill in the historical gaps.

# CHAPTER ONE

Rachel Stewart stood and stretched her neck, wincing at the resulting cracks. Long shadows outside the west-facing storefront let her know she was long past closing shop. She folded her customer's half-sewn dress. Unable to finish her work disappointed her.

Miss Ellie, the store's owner, already suspected the dress wouldn't be finished by tomorrow morning. Unwilling to leave a task for someone else, she planned on coming down after dinner to complete her work.

She stood and went to the door to turn the lock. Weston, Missouri was just as busy during the early evening as any other time. A new surge of settlers heading west after the Civil War gave the city a better purpose these days. She stared at the early evening haze. Any reason was much better than burning other peoples' property just because they might be Confederate sympathizers. Yes, she might be a wee bit bitter still.

Rachel reached for the 'Open' sign and stopped

after a knock at the door. After firmly setting the sign to 'Closed', she turned to the new arrival. The man, a handsome devil, smiled at her. He held up folded fabric with a clear and pleading expression. Spending the day sewing a dress too delicate for her to ever wear left Rachel unwilling to be charitable to anyone. She was tempted to turn him away until tomorrow. Let Miss Ellie help him with whatever he needed.

Except now, the gentleman had his hands together as if begging, the garment under one arm held close to his side. She narrowed her eyes. He used the adorable cowlick in his dark hair, deep brown eyes, and scruff of a dark beard to his advantage. Rachel sighed. He was probably a terror to his mother and any other woman in his life. She turned the lock and opened the door. "Yes?"

He leaned against the door with slight pressure. "Good evening, and thank you for staying open." He pulled the garment from his side, increasing the slight push on the door as he did so. "I need these let out, and your shop is the last one I'll see between here and Fort Dodge."

She smiled at how little he knew of the area. "Oh no, you'll have plenty of places between here and there to hire repairs or alterations." Rachel took the pants he offered. "Nice quality; you can come back tomorrow when the shop's open."

"I can't. We're leaving tomorrow morning."

We? Of course. A man this charming and handsome would be married. He probably had at least five children, one after the other. Rachel sighed, the loneliness of being a spinster a little too true at the moment. She figured his wife was too busy herding their offspring, getting them ready for tomorrow's trip, to sew anything for him. "I see." She opened the door to let him in. "What exactly do you need to be done?"

He stepped in with a grin, waiting until she locked the door. "These are my Sunday pants, and I've outgrown them."

Rachel turned out the waistband to find darts sewn in along the sides. The size would fit a boy, not a full-grown man. "Have they always been yours?"

"Yes. They fit before the war."

She wandered over to her sewing chair and moved her current work before sitting down. "But not after?"

"No. Well, it took a while for me to regain my health." He trailed behind her.

With it being only a little over a year since the Civil War officially ended, Rachel bet hundreds were still healing from the country's wounds. He found a seat by pushing over a book of fabric samples Miss Ellie had created for their customers. The man seemed rather fine to her at the moment, judging by his easy grace. She examined the hem at the end of one of the pant legs. "I'll bet you've grown since then, too."

"I have, but not by much. I was twenty when the war started."

Rachel nodded, doing the math. She'd been fifteen, so they were twenty-five and a newly turned twenty-one now. "In that case, I'll let out the darts and hem before having you try on your pants." She began ripping out the seams.

"Will it take you very long to complete if I need the waist and hems sewn?"

She paused with her seam ripper and glanced up at him with a wry grin. "Not too much. Terribly impatient, aren't you? Sunday isn't for a few more days, you know. Your current pants would be good enough to attend service."

He chuckled. "I am impatient, but not due to church." The man stood and walked to the window while saying, "You're doing me a huge favor by staying late. I don't want to inconvenience you any more than necessary."

Rachel pulled the cut threads free from the fabric. "It's not much effort. The darts are already gone." She stood and went to him, handing him the pants. "There's a changing room under the stairs. Try them on, and we'll see what more needs to be done."

"Yes, ma'am." He took his garment.

She watched as he went to the stairs and realized she'd never asked his name. He glanced back at her with a slight grin before disappearing. Her face grew hot at how he'd caught her staring. Though, to be fair, he had to be used to feminine attention by now. She smiled and went to the sewing machine. Fixing his hems would be fast. His waist might need a quarter-inch dart on each side unless he'd prefer suspenders or a belt.

Rachel removed the green thread and wound in the black. She studied the color for a moment. A dark, almost charcoal gray would be better with the slightly faded material. She went to the spool rack hanging on the wall.

"They're a little long, but the waist fits fine."

She turned to see her customer standing in front of the dressing room door. He had his shirt pulled up enough for her to see a little skin above the beltline. She ignored the budding interest in seeing more of

4

him than politeness allowed and stayed professional. "Have you eaten supper yet?" Rachel asked while walking over to him. "I might need to expand the fit if they're snug."

"They're not too tight. I still have room for growing after dinner tonight." He hooked a thumb into a belt loop and pulled out a little.

Rachel laughed at the idea of this trim man growing paunchy. "I still need to fix your hems on the machine, so adding darts would be simple if you'd like."

Shaking his head, he replied, "I appreciate your offer, but it's getting late, and I only have time for one or the other."

The reminder of the late hour didn't escape her. She had dinner to cook and a project to complete before getting ready for tomorrow. "In that case, change into your prior clothes and I'll get started."

"Yes, ma'am." He gave her a grin with a salute.

By the time she had charcoal gray loaded into her machine, Rachel's customer had reappeared. She reached out for his pants. "Hems are easy and won't take long." She turned one cuff inside out and folded.

He pulled his chair closer to the machine where she worked. "How do you know where to sew without marking it?"

A slammed door from above delayed her response. Isaac would be irritated over her working late tonight. "I made a note of where the fold was while you wore them. Since you were barefoot, I'm allowing a half-inch for your boot heel." She slid the material under the needle.

"Clever. I might have known you'd be crafty."

Her face grew hot at his praise. This close to her, he

smelled like cinnamon with a hint of coffee. "Thank you, but it's just experience. I'm sure you're excellent at what you do as well."

He laughed. "I try to be. I—"

"Rachel! Are you down there?" The stairs creaked as her brother came down them. "Where the hell is supper?" He stopped. "Oh. I didn't know you had a customer."

"Obviously," she muttered and glanced at her customer with a slight grin. He didn't seem happy until returning her smile. The board for the last step gave a groan, and she turned to her brother. "This is my last bit of work for the day." She slid the cuff out from under the sewing machine's needle. "I'd like to introduce my brother, Isaac. Isaac, this is—"

Her customer stood and walked over to Isaac. "Captain Patrick Sinclair. Your sister was kind enough to let me hire alterations after closing time."

After a brief hesitation, Isaac shook his hand. "Oh. A Union soldier, huh? I assume you'll pay for the convenience. Or will you just steal from us as usual?"

The fabric bunched under Rachel's fist. "There's no need to be rude. He'll pay." She stared hard at her brother. "Start the stove's fire for me; I'll be up there as soon as I'm done here."

"Very well." Isaac nodded at their guest. "I'd like to say it's been a pleasure."

"Likewise," Patrick responded.

Isaac frowned. "Rachel, we have a busy day tomorrow."

"I know, I'm hurrying." She slid the second cuff under the needle and muttered, "The sooner you stop yapping, the sooner I'll be done."

"I heard that."

"Don't care," she retorted as the door slammed shut. Isaac's sour attitude toward Union soldiers had been why she'd cheered when he found work. Keeping him busy kept him from bothering customers like Captain Sinclair. "Sorry about his attitude. The war…" She turned the sewing machine's wheel to dip the needle into the fabric

Captain Sinclair leaned back while folding his arms. "That's as good an excuse as anything."

Rachel paused before starting the machine. "Oh? Being bitter about a catastrophic event is an excuse?"

"I meant reason. War is a good reason." He shrugged with a sly grin. "Better?"

She chuckled at his attempt to save the conversation. "Not really better, no, but a good try."

He chuckled. "Sorry. My sweet-talking skills are rusty. The war."

After snorting a laugh, she covered her mouth with a hand before saying, "Why do I think those two words are going to get you out of a lot of trouble with the missus in the future?"

"You might be right." He leaned back in the chair. "I'll add 'find a missus and think up some trouble for her to forgive' to the top of my duty list."

"I see. You have a solid plan, there." She couldn't keep her face from heating after hearing he wasn't married. "Good plan," she added, turning back to her task.

Rachel's sewing machine hummed as she worked the pedal. She peeked at him to find he was staring at her. Her face grew hot at how he smiled when their gazes met. She focused on the hem and struggled to not sneak a peek at him again.

The silence stretched between them until she said, "Isaac isn't usually so short with me, really. He's probably tired and hungry."

'I understand." Patrick leaned forward, closer to Rachel. "I'd be in the same mood if someone was interrupting my evening plans, too."

"Oh, they're not plans so much as a routine." She sewed backward a few stitches to set the thread. "He values customers, just not when the shop has been closed."

"I do apologize for the lateness. You've been more than kind in taking my business."

"How could I resist when you begged me to?" Rachel asked, and pulled the pant leg from the sewing machine. She cut the thread. "It's a simple enough fix and, unlike the dress, something I could do in no time at all."

"The dress? The one you were working on before closing?"

He'd peeked into the shop, then. Rachel hoped he had stopped for her, but knew desperation for a seamstress drove him more than wanting to meet her. "Yes." She began folding his pants and looking for stray threads or possible tears he'd overlooked. "I had to set it aside until after dinner."

"And I apologize again to you and yours about delaying your meal," he said while standing and taking the garment from her. "How much do I owe you?"

"Two bits," Rachel replied. "We have standard rates, and I'm sorry, but Miss Ellie won't allow credit since you won't be in town long."

Patrick grinned. "Smart lady." He dug around in his

pocket. "Does the money go to you?"

Rachel nodded. Working in the shop had rid her of a shyness concerning payment due a long time ago. "Part of it, yes."

"Good. You've done an excellent job."

She stood. "Would you like to try them on and test the length?"

He held the pants against himself for a few seconds before folding them. "I trust your judgment."

She frowned. No one ever took her word the first time. She'd been second-guessed so often, people double-checking her work was a given. "Are you sure? I could be wrong."

Patrick tilted his head and gave her a searching look. "No, I don't think you could be. Your work was fast but precise. I trust your skills."

She took the money. "Thank you, but this is too much for something as simple as ripping stitches and sewing hems. Let me return half at least." Rachel went to the back of the room to the cash box. "There's just enough left in the till to make change out of this."

He waved the hand. "Keep it. You've stayed open late just for me, and I know I've been an inconvenience."

Rachel bit her lip. A dollar fifty was too much for the work she'd done, yet every little bit helped. "If you're sure?"

"I am. You've made an ordinary errand more enjoyable."

She closed the money box and slid it back under the counter. They both had things to do this evening. Still, she didn't want to say goodbye to him just yet. Rachel walked up to him, searching for anything to talk about and keep him there longer. "I don't suppose with a name like yours you're anything but Irish."

He smiled. "We're Scottish, but we've been here long enough to be all American."

She nodded and said, "So have we."

"Scottish or American?"

"Both," Rachel replied and followed him to the door. "Stewarts have been here since the country's beginning. We've fought in every war since."

"Your brother, too?" Patrick asked while pausing to lean against the doorframe. "I assume his limp is from a war wound?"

"He and our father were injured." She didn't want to introduce their mourning into the conversation, but couldn't omit the worst. "Isaac continues to improve over time, but Pa didn't recover."

"Sorry for your loss."

She unlocked the door for him. "Thank you. It was a dark time for everyone, I'm afraid."

"I agree." He glanced out the window for a moment before turning to look at her. "I should go. We have an early morning tomorrow and a long day ahead. Plus, Mr. Stewart is waiting for his meal."

Rachel chuckled at the reminder. "I'd hoped he'd take the initiative and start cooking for us both. But you're right. Tomorrow is an early day for us, as well. I hope you have safe travels."

He lingered at the threshold for a second before stepping outside. "So do I."

She closed the door behind him. Rachel watched for a moment while Patrick crossed the street. He'd have to hurry if he planned on reaching Fort Leavenworth by dark. She turned the lock, wishing they had tomorrow together. She'd love to know more about his life. To be honest, she'd like just listening to him talk about anything he wanted to. Any other time, she'd have found a way to keep him talking a little longer.

She continued to watch as he reached a few horses tied up to a hitching post. Patrick looked toward the shop at her. Rachel smiled while hoping he couldn't see her. He grinned and gave a slight salute before getting onto his animal. Her face burned even as she chuckled over being caught. She liked how the attraction wasn't so one-sided. Maybe she could talk Isaac into setting up shop in Fort Dodge instead of Santa Fe.

"I'd better go see what he's doing," she said to herself. Rachel picked up the half-finished dress and climbed the stairs. Isaac couldn't be cooking, or she'd smell something burning by now.

Isaac fed the wood stove's small fire while squatted in front of the oven. "Did you finally get rid of the Yank?"

"Yes, and I'm sad to see him go."

He snorted. "I'll bet. He's a pretty boy."

"Stop right there with your teasing." She put the dress on the table and went to him. "Captain Sinclair is a good man, not like those other Union soldiers. He tipped me a dollar and a half for my troubles."

His eyebrows rose, and he ignored the stove for a moment. "All that for a little bit of sewing? Did you ask what else he might need? He could have stayed for dinner at least. Home cooking and all."

"No, he couldn't." Rachel walked over to their one comfy chair. She paused and then better arranged the dress over the arm so no one would sit on the threaded needle. "I didn't ask because he's gone tomorrow."

"Eh. Too bad." He stood slowly as if his knees were paining him again. "Do you know where? I wouldn't be averse to following if he were dropping silver dollars along the way."

She chuckled at the idea. "I have a feeling he's not as loose with his money as all that. Otherwise, he'd have had a new pair of trousers sewn instead of an old pair mended."

"Eh. I like my plan better, letting you hold your apron under his pockets to let the coins fall."

"All of your joking is useless. He's gone tomorrow, as are we." She took the last bit of butter from the icebox. "We'll never see him again."

# CHAPTER TWO

Patrick lifted the brim of his cavalry hat and wiped his brow. The setting sun hovered over the horizon. Golden light bounced off of the overhead clouds. The warm reflection lit the shadows caused by the surrounding buildings and trees of Fort Leavenworth,

He'd left the hat hanging from its necktie on his saddle's pommel while in the seamstress' shop. He grinned. Miss Stewart had been a dream the entire time he'd waited for his repairs. She looked like an angel and sewed like a demon. The gleaming yellow in the sunlight reminded him of her hair. Her blue eyes mirrored the early evening sky. If her lips were a little less rosy and more twilight coral, every late afternoon would remind him of her. Too bad he and his men were moving out tomorrow for a new assignment. A few more days here and he'd insist on his men refreshing their wardrobes just for her financial benefit.

He nodded at a passing soldier. The slow and easy walk of his horse didn't bother Patrick. The quiet time gave him a chance to dwell more on the seamstress. Growing up, he'd been close enough to his sister, Josie, to recognize how Rachel had a much older dress than most of the women around Weston. The latest fashions worn by the few officers' wives this far west hadn't been what tipped him off. Instead, the thin fabric with the repairs only visible close up showed him how much she'd done without in the past few years.

Everyone around here suffered, except for those swooping in to take advantage of desperate people. Patrick ignored his protective instincts. Most likely she was one of many ladies working in town, and would be fine with her brother there. She didn't need any soldier loitering around her.

Cottonwood trees rustled in the breeze coming off the Missouri River as he rode alongside the water. Rachel's brother's gruffness nagged at him. The fellow had been kind enough to her, so Patrick had ignored his protective instincts at the time. Rachel shone like a star; however, her brother, similar in coloring to her, gloomed like a dark comet. A cranky, smart-mouthed comet.

On the other hand, he mused, her retorts toward Isaac were amusing. Patrick would love to get into arguing with her sometime just to see what she'd say next. But doing so meant going back to Weston instead of Fort Dodge. Nothing else would kill his Army career faster than staying put when the military said go.

Patrick dismounted in front of Fort Leavenworth's main stable. He nodded at the stable hand. "Thank you," he'd said to the soldier caring for the animal.

"You're welcome, sir."

He hadn't worn his uniform into town. No matter what side they'd been on, some of the residents held resentment toward any soldier, Union or Confederate. Patrick had wanted to get there, accomplish his errands, and return without any sort of incident. He retrieved the packages and his clothes from the saddlebag. "Did I miss dinner?"

"Just about." The young man pulled the saddle from Patrick's horse. "The kitchen might be open."

"Appreciate it." He set off for the officers' quarters and the small mess hall there. If he could charm the cook out of leftovers, he wouldn't need to make a meal of his dried fruit and pecans.

The aroma of roast chicken lingered in the air as he stepped inside the building. "Hello?" he hollered when reaching the end of the hall. "Anybody have scraps for me?"

"Again, Captain Sinclair?" The largish woman, old enough to be his mother, came out from the kitchen and wiped her hands on her apron. "I've just washed the last dish."

He strolled up to her. "Aw, come on, Molly. You know I'm leaving tomorrow."

She turned on her heel with a "Hmph," and walked back into the kitchen. From inside the room, her voice echoed as she added, "Put your things away and come on in. I'll rustle something up for ya."

Patrick left the hall, agreeable to anything if she fed him. He crossed the courtyard to the bachelor officers' quarters. In his room, he put his hat and purchases on his bunk. With most of the troops out fighting the natives, he had his own room. The solid walls, door, and comfortable bed weren't things he'd ever take for granted again. He ran his fingers down the quilt his mother had made for him. There'd be plenty of time to think after dinner. Right now, his stomach ached.

Hurrying back, he paused to return a salute and continued on into the mess hall. Molly waited for him in the doorway, her foot tapping. He smiled at her mock outrage. She was always blustering, yet managed to keep him fed. Her cooking was why he'd met Rachel today. "I appreciate your saving me back some dinner."

She smacked his shoulder with a hand towel as he walked by her. "Enough to clean up my kitchen when you're done?"

He sat at the table closest to the stove. "Yes, ma'am."

"We ran out of gravy. Jenkins had more than his share." Molly set down two plates of chicken and mashed potatoes.

Patrick took the fork she handed him. "Considerate of him."

"Yes, well, I knew he'd have a heavy go with the ladle." She shrugged. "Teaches me to not save some back when he's at the table."

He nodded, preoccupied with the buttery potatoes and how good they tasted. "Excellent, as usual, and I don't blame Jenkins after all."

She wiped her mouth. "So, what kept you out so late? Leavenworth City rolls up its streets pretty early unless you're on the wrong side of town."

"I was in Weston, having some pants mended." He broke up a biscuit and took a bite. The warm bread soon melted the fresh butter. Patrick hummed in happiness, almost happy at the lack of gravy.

"You went to Ellie's for the work?" she asked, and Patrick nodded. Molly shifted in her seat. "Good choice. Rachel Stewart is a hidden treasure, and I don't know what El will do when she's gone."

He paused in buttering another biscuit. "She's going somewhere?"

"She and her brother are. Last week, Miss Ellie placed an advert for a new employee."

Patrick almost said she shouldn't need to follow her brother, but held back. Likely those two were the only family they had left. If they went along the same trail as him to anywhere near Fort Dodge, he'd get a chance to see her again. He set down the butter knife. "Any idea where they've decided to go?"

"I hadn't heard. Maybe back east, or even the west coast." She ate her last bite. "Isaac has been itching to leave the area for months and has been pushing at Rachel to leave with him. I don't blame either one for wanting to start anew. Their family farm was destroyed during the General Order Number Eleven incident."

Most people knew about the order designed to punish Confederate bushwhackers living in four Missouri counties. The plan backfired. Resentment boiled under the surface, still. Patrick figured the people would take decades to recover. "That's a shame," was all he could say, since he'd hate anyone associated with the area troops, too. "Do you know what happened to the Stewarts in particular?"

She shrugged. "A little, and about the same as everyone else in those counties. Their farm was burned while Isaac and Mr. Stewart were gone, fighting in the war. Mrs. Stewart and Rachel lined up with the others along the Missouri River. Steamboat captains picked them up, all of them, and the Stewarts landed in Weston. Miss Ellie and Mrs. Stewart had been in elementary school together."

He ate up the last bit of his dinner. "Did Mr. and Mrs. Stewart rebuild their farm?" Patrick asked, and dreaded the answer he suspected he already knew.

"No. He died on some battlefield. I forget which one. She passed away two years ago after a long illness." Molly stood, taking their dishes. "If you ask me, her heart broke when her husband died and having to see her son's spirit gone."

Isaac's bitterness came to Patrick's mind, and he had to disagree while he followed her into the kitchen to learn more. "He seemed pretty spirited to me."

She dunked the dishes into the washtub and began scrubbing. "You met him, too?"

He nodded, taking a dripping plate from her. "Briefly. He doesn't care for Union soldiers despite the fact he was one."

"After the General Order destroyed his family? I don't blame him."

"Neither do I." Taking the second wet dish from her, Patrick asked, "Were most people around here affected by the order?"

"Somewhat, even if they didn't have farms in those counties. The process started out orderly but soon disintegrated into a free for all. Not all soldiers were bad, but not all were good, either."

He nodded and took the forks to dry them. "We might have to wait for a generation or two for the country's scars to fade." Patrick tapped the washbasin. "Do you want me to empty the water?"

Molly made shooing motions with her hands. "I'll take care of this. You're leaving tomorrow, remember?"

"I don't mind helping."

"No, go on. Get some rest before tomorrow morning. I've chatted your ear off about people you'll never meet again."

Patrick forced a smile. He'd spent as many as thirty minutes with Rachel. Yet his heart sank at how he might never see her again. Molly didn't know where the Stewarts were moving, and if he asked to stay at Fort Leavenworth to find out? His army career would end like a snowball hitting the general's face. Especially if he explained why. "You're right. I'd better turn in for the evening."

"Goodnight, Captain. See you tomorrow at breakfast."

"Goodnight." He headed out and to the officers' quarters. Other soldiers passed him, and he nodded a greeting at each. Most of the men he'd led during the war were back in Virginia or already at various forts scattered throughout the wilderness. There'd been a few friends he'd made during one of his darkest times. None of them had survived.

He opened the door to his room. Tomorrow meant proving himself to the tougher nuts on their way to Fort Dodge. The trip west would give him plenty of time to think about and come to terms with the past.

Patrick moved his things off of the bed and onto a small end table. Fresh water and a small wash basin with a hand towel sat on a dresser. He began scrubbing his face, lost in thought over the Stewarts. He'd heard about families torn apart during the Civil

War. Whether by incidents or intent, he had cousins he'd never see again. Still, his parents and sister's new family were together back in Pennsylvania. He could visit them any time the military allowed him.

Rachel and Isaac were on their own, without any other kin if they lived above a shop. He undressed, folding his clothes and packing them in the haversack. Tomorrow meant returning to his cavalry uniform along with no time to run back to Weston just to see Rachel. He'd love to learn where she was going. Not that he could follow, but even a letter or two exchanged between them would be interesting.

He settled into bed, the ropes under the straw tick mattress squeaking with his weight. Part of being a soldier, particularly an officer, meant the army dictated his life. Patrick had always been fine with following orders until today. Now, he'd like to loiter in Fort Leavenworth for the morning at least and visit the lovely seamstress he'd met today.

# CHAPTER THREE

"Isaac, the sun's up already." Rachel shook her brother with her free hand. The man would sleep all day every day if she'd let him. "Come on. I want to be somewhere before tonight."

"Mmph," he groaned. "Do you have to be so loud?" He rolled over, pulling the covers over his head.

She hadn't bothered starting a fire in the stove but now reconsidered. Coffee was the only thing luring him out of bed most days. "You've seen the illustrations of Santa Fe as well as I have." Rachel resumed making checkmarks on her packing list. "I don't know how you could lie there and not be ready to go."

"Those mountains aren't going anywhere," he said, his voice muffled under the comforter.

"Neither are you at this rate." Satisfied for the moment about her to-do list, she examined the room one last time. They each had their own bedroom in her dreams. They'd live in a place big enough to give them privacy instead of a single room, with a parlor, kitchen, and washroom. Motivation renewed, she pushed at him again. "Upsie-daisy so I can fold your bedding."

"Don't bother." He flipped over, his face framed by their mother's quilt. "I'll do it myself and hitch up Bossy when you're ready to leave."

She was ready now but didn't believe he was, judging by how snug he was under the covers. "Your things are all packed in your one bag?"

"As many as I want to take." He flung the blankets off and sat up fully dressed. "See? Sleeping in your clothes is very efficient."

A knock at the door interrupted Rachel's next argument. "Hello? Have you left yet?"

She hollered, "No, Miss Ellie. We'll be along soon. You know Isaac."

"Very well, dear."

Rachel turned to her brother. "Now?"

"Yeah." He rubbed his eyes. "Let's get going, so it'll all be over soon."

He wore his maudlin attitude like a favorite shirt, but she wasn't fooled at all. The trip west had been his idea and, once she warmed up to leaving Missouri behind, hers as well. Only, now she might not mind staying… Rachel shook her head. No handsome brown-eyed soldier was going to change her mind. She'd be a successful business owner in Santa Fe, sewing new dresses for all the recent women settlers. She and her brother couldn't be the only ones looking for a better life away from the east.

Isaac took the coffee pot from the cold stove. "I wouldn't mind roasting a few coffee beans for chewing on in the morning."

"Something to get you moving so you can get moving?" She grabbed her small carpet bag. "I'll write down to cook up a few tonight at our campfire." Rachel scribbled the task before tossing the book and pencil into her bag.

He nodded and opened the door. "Exactly."

Rachel followed Isaac down the stairs, leaving what had been their home for the past year. Part of her, the one afraid of change, wanted to stay safe. The rest of her wanted to push her brother out of the way and lead the way west. She paced herself and took each step one at a time. "How far do you think we'll go today?"

He stared up at her until she stood next to him. "Probably ten or fifteen miles since it's our first day." He opened the door to the shop's showroom. "Settlers west could reach twenty miles a day with a loaded-down wagon. I'd like it if we could go further."

His goal seemed almost impossible. "Good thing for Bossy we're traveling light."

Isaac stopped. "Speaking of her, I'll go hitch her up before saying goodbye to Miss Ellie."

Her nose stung and her eyes grew watery. She understood his need to put off seeing her friend and their benefactor. "It'll be difficult."

"Isn't everything?"

She laughed at his typical morose response. "I suppose so. Life is but a veil of tears."

Isaac grinned. "Now you're learning," he quipped and went out the back door.

Rachel shook her head at his teasing. He didn't fool her. Isaac relied on her sunny nature to lift his depression. He always switched to cheery when life made her too sad to smile. She sighed and looked at the back entrance to the shop room. Time to say goodbye to her boss and benefactor.

The hinges creaked as she pushed open the swinging door. "Miss Ellie?"

"There you are." The middle-aged woman stood up from the sewing machine and walked up to Rachel. "I have something for you, and you're not allowed to refuse." She held out an envelope. "Something to help along your next adventure."

Rachel took the offering and peeked into the unsealed envelope. More cash than she'd seen together in years, maybe forever, lay inside. The bills might be small, but there were so many of them. "I can't take this. It's your profits for the year, at least."

"You can. Put the money in your pocket, deep, and be glad about having emergency funds." When Rachel hesitated, Miss Ellie pushed the envelope closer to her. "Don't argue and don't tell Isaac until you're too far to turn around."

She nodded, unable to argue with her boss. "Yes, ma'am."

Miss Ellie brought her in for a hug. "No ma'aming me now, missy. You're on your own with that mangy brother of yours, now."

"I heard that."

The ladies stopped hugging, and Miss Ellie went to Isaac. "Come here and give me one last hug goodbye."

He did as she requested. "This isn't the last goodbye, you know. We'll be back someday."

"Maybe so." Miss Ellie let go of him. "And you might love the wild west so much you never return." She sniffed and smoothed her skirt. "I might have to come to visit and make sure you're doing well."

"You might have to." He glanced at Rachel, his grin fading. "Ready?"

"Yes." She gave Miss Ellie one last hug, as did Isaac. "The day isn't getting any younger." The three of them went out the back to the stable. Now that she faced the wagon, the bed seemed terribly sparse for a two-month trip west.

"Sure you have enough provisions?" Miss Ellie asked, barely tall enough to peer into the back of the wagon.

"I'll hunt and fish on the way there," he said while climbing onto the wagon's seat.

Rachel nodded and let him pull her up beside him. "Plus there are hotels along the way. Not that we'll stop often, but between them and the trading posts we should be fine."

After a *hmph*, Miss Ellie walked to the front of the wagon. "I suppose you know what you're doing. Just don't spend all your money by the time you get to Fort Larned. I don't want to have to ride a stagecoach out there to tan your hides."

Rachel laughed at the idea, but could imagine the woman making good on her promise. "We won't. I have a budget, plus a little nest egg I don't plan on using."

Miss Ellie grinned, her hands on her hips. "Good. You two write when you get to Santa Fe. Let me know you made it there safe."

"Will do, and thank you, ma'am." Isaac rubbed his nose and sniffed. "We consider you family."

"In that case, don't ma'am me and get going already or we'll all be crying." She wiped her eyes. "I have a business to run. No time for tears."

He snapped the reins and Bossy began pulling them out of the small stable-yard. Rachel turned and waved until she couldn't see Miss Ellie anymore. She faced the front with a little shiver. The morning sun's light and warmth didn't reach the street just yet. The chilly air held a hint of frost. "Do you think we're starting too late in the year?"

"I wondered about that, too." He moved the reins to one hand and scratched his chin for a moment. "Two months isn't a long time. It'll be over before we know it."

Rachel sat and watched the closed doors pass by them, the streets just starting to stir with people. She tried and failed to suppress the urge to ask, "And your friend will hire you?"

"Yes." Isaac nudged her shoulder with his. "And before you ask again, remember the letter from last week?"

She knew he was right, but still. Nothing ever remained the same over time. Otherwise, they'd be on the Stewart family farm with their parents. "All right. I won't worry."

They rolled along for a few minutes before he added, "I don't blame you for fretting. This is the furthest you've been from home. I was scared, too."

She wanted to deny being nervous, but he was right. She was. So many what-ifs loomed large in her mind. Indian attacks, getting lost out in the middle of the plains, their old wagon falling apart were all possible before they even reached their first campsite. She had a guidebook and hoped the information was still accurate despite the publication date.

They rolled past farms with new buildings and crops harvested or ready to harvest. The leaves hadn't begun turning despite the crisp air. Fog lingered in the lower-lying areas, pools of water from a recent rain under them.

By the time they reached the ferry crossing for the Missouri River, she had realized neither had said a word in the few miles between here and Weston. Fort Leavenworth lay across the water, some of the buildings newer than others. The fort reminded her of how Patrick had mentioned leaving early in the morning.

Rachel bit her lip. A soldier's idea of early might be different from hers. She should have told him they'd be going in the same direction. He wouldn't have stalled on her account. Still, she'd like to see if he found excuses to find her along the way.

"My bet is Captain Sinclair is already gone, if you're wondering," Isaac said.

She cut her eyes to him. He always had a way of knowing what was on her mind. "I wasn't thinking about him."

"Uh-huh. He's probably a West Point graduate. Most officers are."

Certain she had already lost the denial argument, Rachel answered, "I didn't even consider his history."

"Sure you didn't. No woman would give a second thought about a pretty boy army officer."

He had her there. Any woman with eyes would be swooning over Captain Sinclair, in Rachel's opinion. She didn't want to go over her attraction for him with anyone, especially Isaac, so she countered with, "You sound horribly jealous right now. Are you fishing for compliments or just grumpy this morning?"

He chuckled. "Maybe a little of both. I saw guys like him have it easy during the war. We did all the work and officers got all the glory." Isaac gave her a side glance. "The ladies liked them a little more, too."

"Hmm." Rachel's stomach twisted. She was hungry. Had to be, because the thought of Patrick with anyone else didn't bother her at all. She barely knew the man. He seemed nice and all. She had no reason to care about his past loves while at war. "I can't imagine why. Every man is different, yet they're all the same."

Isaac laughed and shook his head. "Maybe, but some are thought of as better than others, and nothing we think is going to change that."

"Still. I like Captain Sinclair because he pays well for services," she began, and frowned when her brother snorted a laugh. "Don't be rude. And he knows how to behave, unlike you."

"True. I have no idea how to behave in polite society." He hopped down and walked up to the ferryman to pay the fee. "I'll be right back." Isaac settled up with the man then got back on the wagon. "Expensive, but worth it."

She nodded. They didn't own much between them, and she wanted to keep what little they had. Isaac guided the wagon onto the ferry. Before long, they took off across the wide river. "I remember we crossed here before the war."

"Mm-hm. Pa wanted to go just to show us the other side. He always wanted to explore."

The river stretched out on either side of them, a broad blue ribbon. Crossing now seemed a lot longer over a smaller body of water. She sighed into the crisp mid-morning breeze. Even mountains changed given enough time. The war had taken so much from everyone. No one could be the same now. Isaac came back different—harder, sadder—and had lost his boyish sense of fun.

He caught her looking at him and grinned. "What happens when Santa Fe isn't far enough west for us?"

She laughed. "Then we learn to dig for gold in California."

Isaac tipped his hat at the ferryman. He clicked at Bossy, and their wagon lumbered over the wooden slats. The wheels hit the ground with a bump. "Better get used to rough roads. I have a feeling we're in the most civilized part."

"We could stay at a fort if something bad happens," she offered, and frowned when her brother laughed.

"I figured we could if a certain captain invited us… I mean, invited you."

She held on to the seat as Bossy climbed out of the river valley. "You know I wouldn't go somewhere safe without you and, besides, I don't know anyone who might ask me to stay."

They crested the top, and he nudged her shoulder. "No? Then who's that?"

# CHAPTER FOUR

Rachel looked where Isaac pointed. A group of soldiers rode up to their right, with several wagons trailing behind them. Captain Sinclair grabbed her attention in an instant. He was wearing his full uniform and rode a bay horse. Her palms grew a little sweaty.

"I'll wait until they ride on and we'll follow since I'm sure we're slower. You're catching flies."

She closed her mouth with a snap but didn't stop staring. "I haven't seen so many soldiers at one time since the night we lost the farm."

"Lucky you."

"I know." Rachel watched as Captain Sinclair, she couldn't think of him as Patrick, rode past the troops as if inspecting them. "I suppose this won't be the last time we see the military. Especially around the forts."

"I almost hope we're swimming in them." He shrugged when she glanced at him. "We'll be riding through dangerous territory. The natives attack sometimes, and I'd rather someone else take the arrow instead of us."

She looked at Captain Sinclair again. He'd been through the war. Indians wouldn't dare attack him. "I'd rather no one is killed."

After a pause, Isaac said, "Me too."

Watching the captain work, Rachel smiled. No matter what her brother groused about, she loved watching the handsome man in his element. He rode as if born on a horse, his pants a sun-bleached shade of blue lighter than his jacket. He had on a white shirt, and she'd bet it wasn't the same one he'd worn into the shop last evening.

He glanced at her and Rachel's heart skipped a beat. Then he looked at her again with a smile. She couldn't help but grin back at him, and kept her hands clasped in her lap to keep from waving. He turned to another soldier next to him. When the man gave the nod, Captain Sinclair nudged his horse into a trot towards them.

He tipped his hat. "What a pleasant surprise. Are you two here to say goodbye to me and the men?"

Isaac snorted, and Rachel ignored her brother. She smiled at Patrick. "Not quite. This is just a happy accident. We're moving to Santa Fe."

His eyebrows rose in surprise. "Because you'll be closer to me at Fort Dodge?"

She chuckled and tried to not bat her eyelashes at him. "Sorry to say, no. I'd need more than one night to consider chucking everything to follow a man west."

"Ah, well, I'd hoped you might be smitten with my charm." He gave her a rakish grin. "My mistake."

"Why do I think there's another army of women who've done just that?" His puzzled expression led her to add, "Leaving everything behind to follow you anywhere, I mean."

He grinned at her. "I've never noticed anyone who has. You'll let me know if a band of women is following me, won't you? I wouldn't want to neglect any lovely ladies susceptible to my charms."

"Certainly. I'll be first in line to tell you all about them," she said while shaking her head no.

Patrick chuckled. "Good. I'll always enjoy your chatting with me." He tipped his hat. "Miss, sir. I look forward to seeing more of you both in the weeks ahead."

"As do we, I, yes." Rachel cleared her throat. "Likewise, sir."

Heat flared in his expression before he nodded. "Till then."

As he rode away, she watched, entranced by his air of command. He seemed so sure of himself. Everything about him was like a dessert she couldn't get enough of. Rachel sighed. The man was adorable.

"So, are we ready to continue on our way? I'd like to get somewhere today."

She glared at her brother. "Don't even begin to blame me for chatting with Captain Sinclair."

He chuckled and clicked at Bossy as the last of the army wagons rolled on past them. "He seemed pretty happy to be chatting with you, too. Thus, I blame him for the delay."

The captain did seem pleased to see her. The second glance he gave when recognizing her warmed Rachel's heart, too. Her toes curled in her shoes. "Do you think so? Or was he just being polite?"

"Polite is a nod and a tip of the hat before refocusing on the task. Happy is trotting over to you for a howdy-do."

"To both of us."

"Yeah, I'm pretty sure he was coming over here for you, darlin'. I'm good-looking, but you're pretty." He glanced at her before returning his attention to the road. "The man is as interested in you as you are him." Isaac shook his head. "I'll have to keep the shotgun loaded."

The idea of both men creeping around, one to visit her the other to shoot him, amused her and she laughed. "We'll see. My vanity wants to believe you, but we'll see."

Wanting to direct him away from her interests, Rachel pointed ahead. "Can you see through the trees? It looks like there's a large valley ahead. Maybe it's the beginning of the plains."

"Possibly. Seems a bit too soon, though."

They wound around a hill, the wide field falling to their side. A farmhouse and barn stood in the middle. Cows milled around, grazing. Rachel missed the life she would have had and turned her sights to the future. Santa Fe had to be better.

The day wore on. Neither talked much. Rachel had spent most of her days in the past couple of years at a sewing machine, so she was used to being quiet. The wheels rolling along the busted-up clay ground made a soothing rhythm. Being too excited to sleep last night left her drowsy now. "Did we want to stop for a noon meal or push on through to supper?"

"I'd like to see how far we get today." He glanced at her. "Even if it means we play tag with the army up ahead."

She nodded, liking the idea of loitering around the

country with Captain Sinclair. Even better was the protection he and his men offered to them, even if only by their proximity. "I have a jar we could use for water and could eat a couple of biscuits."

"Good. We'll stop at the next creek."

"Upstream from the soldiers, I hope. Some of them seemed to smell a bit, and I'm not drinking their bathwater."

Isaac laughed. "Yes. We'll hurry past the next time they stop just for you." He nudged her with his shoulder. "But not too fast, because I know you'll want to gawk at Captain Handsome."

Rachel's face burned at his teasing. He wasn't wrong, though. She sighed. The man was easy on the eyes. "He seems to be Captain Charming, too. I'll bet he wouldn't have let the other soldiers use our chickens for target practice."

Isaac stayed quiet. She knew he wanted to rebut. Previously, he'd argue about most soldiers being wrong no matter what side they'd been on. Unwilling to dwell on the past, she tried to ignore the army group parked where the creek meandered closer to the road. Rachel stared ahead as she and Isaac passed them.

Captain Sinclair caught her eye, but she didn't turn her head. Even when he tipped his hat, she gave a slight nod but didn't look at him. She also ignored her brother's dig into her ribs. "Stop it," she hissed. "We're not going to make a fuss every time I see him."

"Fine, but you're taking all of the fun out of running into the man."

She couldn't help but take a peek at the captain. Their eyes met, and he smiled at her before turning to another officer. She faced the front again with a smile of her own. Isaac might be right after all. He might be as smitten with her as she was with him.

"We'll go on up a ways. The water should be clearer. You can get a full jar of water before we take off again."

"I like your plan," she replied, and they rolled on for a little while. As soon as he pulled off to the side, Rachel gathered her skirts and hopped down. She followed the path to the creek as Isaac unhitched Bossy for her drink, too.

The water made soft sounds as it flowed over the rocks. The forests had been giving way to more considerable stretches of prairie grass. Soon, if the guidebook was accurate, there would be nothing but plains stretching in every direction.

She stepped down to the water's edge. The bank seemed solid, if a little squishy. Rachel put her foot down, lost her balance, and fell into the water with a scream.

# CHAPTER FIVE

Everyone's heads, including Patrick's, turned to the west. Rachel and her brother had rolled on ahead, and that was a woman's scream. He told Lambert, his first officer, "Let's go."

The officer barked an order to stay as Patrick jumped on his horse. They rode to the Stewarts' wagon and stopped in time to see a drenched Rachel step out from the water's tree line. He hopped down and hurried to her. "Ma'am? Are you all right? Where's Mr. Stewart?"

"I'm fine. Cold, and now embarrassed over you two seeing me, but fine. Isaac is letting Bossy get a drink."

Rachel's cheeks glowed bright red, and water still dripped from her golden hair. Her blue eyes flashed with anger when he laughed. Patrick felt terrible, but still. She was awfully pretty even soaking wet. "I'm sorry, truly, but all of the worst-case scenarios went through my mind at your scream."

"Yes, I suppose I'd laugh at you, too," she said while wiping water from her face.

The first officer piped up. "I know I would."

Patrick gave him a glare he knew the man wouldn't take seriously this time. "You do have something else to do, don't you?"

"Yes, sir, I do." Still grinning, he turned his horse and went back to their group.

He turned to Rachel. "I'm sure a seamstress has plenty of dry clothes to wear. Would you like help?" Her eyes widened, and he verbally backpedaled. "I mean, maybe I can fetch you a blanket or two?"

"You know how the cobbler's children have no shoes?" she asked him while wringing out her apron. "I'll need to change into my Sunday dress until this one dries." Rachel looked up at him with a smile. "The creek is rather cold for bathing. I'm spoiled and usually heat my water and use soap."

"I don't blame you. There have been enough cold baths in my life. Too many, in fact."

"During the war?"

He hesitated, unwilling to talk about some of the worst conditions he'd faced. "Exclusively, yes. Now I heat water whenever possible, and sometimes when impossible." She laughed at his quip and Patrick decided he'd never heard anything so appealing. He'd have to ask Lieutenant Lambert for more jokes later. "You said your brother is around here?"

She began unwinding her hair and started squeezing out the water. "Yes, close by. Probably at the creek, wondering how I managed to fall in."

"Good. I'd rather you not be alone out here."

Rachel chuckled and shook her head. "I shouldn't be, obviously."

"Accidents happen." A curl escaped when she

scooped her hair into a loose bun. Patrick wanted nothing more than to undo her actions and comb the strands with his fingers. He cleared his throat, needing to say anything to divert his imagination. "I've seen worse. You didn't twist your ankle or break your wrist."

"No, the water broke my fall even if it's not as soft as one might think."

He grinned and crossed his arms to resist the need to hug her. "Let me know whether any part of you aches more than other. We have a doctor with us, so there's no need for you to suffer."

Rachel looked behind her and leaned closer to him. "I might need a poultice for my dignity."

"I'll get right on that, ma'am," he said. Isaac and their horse crashing through the brush to them distracted him from her sparkling blue eyes. Patrick greeted him with, "Stewart."

Isaac nodded. "Sinclair. She's fine. Merely a tumble into the creek."

"So I've learned." Patrick mounted his horse and tipped his hat at Rachel. "Ma'am. Glad you're well. I'll see you later."

"Thank you for checking. My fall could have been something more serious."

"I'm glad it wasn't." Taking note of Isaac's glare, he turned his horse and began riding back. Stewart was damned annoying, but Patrick couldn't blame him. He'd have done the same when Josie fell in love with her husband. Only being in a Confederate prison camp had stopped him.

He raised his chin and pushed the ordeal to the back of his mind where it belonged. His life now was taking command of a frontier fort, not living in the past. Lambert came up to him, and Patrick asked, "Are we ready?"

"Yes, sir. I assume the lady is well?"

"She is. Just took a fall into the creek."

The junior officer grinned as they both turned their horses toward the main group of men. "I'm glad it wasn't anything more serious."

"So am I," Patrick replied. As Lambert went on about their status and how he'd procured a lunch for him, he tried to pay attention. All he wanted to do was go back to Rachel and ignore her brother while they talked. If he were honest, he'd admit to wanting to mention some of his achievements just to impress her. Maybe clean up some of the jokes he'd heard in the military so she'd smile at him again.

"...the Indians carried off Jenkins in a knapsack as well. We threw a blanket party for Rogers because he wasn't keeping watch."

"Excuse me? What did you say?"

"Nothing. I'm talking gibberish to see how long you'd be thinking about that little ol' gal."

Patrick chuckled at how he referred to Rachel. "I see. You didn't consider I might be going over the logistics of getting us from here to Dodge?"

"I have eyes, and she's a pretty woman. Most of us noticed her until you went over to talk to her at the Missouri."

"Until then?"

"Yep." He shrugged. "She's taken with you, too. None of us has a chance."

"I don't reckon Miss Stewart is as interested as you think. She's merely polite." The words sounded like a lie even to his own ears.

The lieutenant gave him a hard look. "I see. Earlier, you'd said you met her yesterday evening?"

"Yes, I haven't known her long at all. Thus, she is a kind and impartial lady." Wanting to refocus the other man's attention, he pointed at the troops. "Are we ready to continue? I'd like to make up for lost time."

"Yes, they're loitering. I'll go put a boot to their butts."

"Very well." He tried not to smile as the officer made good on his promise and rode off in the men's direction. Lambert was from the South but had fought hard for the Union. Patrick liked having the best assisting officer in the army with him. Even if he teased a little too much about Rachel.

The rest of the day went according to plan. A little too routine for comfort. Patrick wasn't used to an easy time of moving troops anywhere. Still, he couldn't complain when they arrived at a wide spot to camp at Stranger Creek without incident.

Plenty of daylight was left, and he could press on. Patrick stared out at the rolling hills to the west. Their peaks and valleys had kept Rachel out of his sight most of the afternoon. If he pushed the troops faster, everyone would guess keeping up with her was the cause for their discomfort. The men and their trip to the next assignment was his priority, he reminded his feelings. Not chasing after a woman with the sweetest face he'd ever seen.

He smiled when thinking of her accident this morning. She'd been so pretty even in disarray. Patrick had a feeling he'd like her even more disheveled and ignored the desire filling his veins. Dwelling on her right now would lead to nothing but frustration. Instead, he focused on getting to Fort Dodge and what his assignment would be once there.

The United States government wanted the citizens protected from attacks from all sides. Indians, Mormons, resentful Mexicans were all threatening settlers. He looked forward to fighting people who weren't as much of an American as he was. They would learn a solid lesson in how to treat a young and strong country like theirs.

"Sir."

He turned to Lambert. "Yes?"

"The scout says a good place to camp for the night is five miles ahead. Do we want to continue there or have him go further?"

Using backward planning, Patrick figured they would have sunlight to do chores by but only barely. "We'll go to where he suggests."

"Yes, sir."

As the young man rode forward, Patrick regretted not having an officer of equal status among the soldiers with him. His first officer was easy to work with, yet he missed the comradery of several in his rank. This wasn't wartime. He couldn't break protocol and be chummy with anyone here, or he'd be accused of favoritism.

He lifted his hat to wipe his brow. The leaves showed the barest hint of yellow. A wet dew hung in the humid air. Winter wasn't his favorite season, but he wouldn't mind an ice-cold drink. If the water at camp was anywhere near warm, he'd just as soon have tea.

The first officer hadn't offered, and Patrick hadn't

asked about the scout mentioning the Stewarts. Judging by the amount of kidding around Lambert had given him, teasing would have been the man's priority over supplies at camp tonight. He couldn't blame the guy. Patrick hoped he'd have the chance to return the favor to him someday. Everyone deserved someone who loved them.

A little trickle of fear flowed through Patrick. Not that anyone loved anyone. No siree. He might be smitten by a pretty lady who seemed to like him, but there was no love. After a glance around to see if anyone saw the expression on his face, he relaxed in the saddle. There was a reason he never played poker. His thoughts shone out like a lighthouse on a clear night.

It'd be better if he thought about securing the supplies they brought along for the various forts between here and Dodge. They'd have to be sure Indians didn't come by and steal everything they had. Patrick couldn't blame them for wanting tools, construction materials, and food. They lived off of the land, and from what he saw the area out here needed a lot of civilization to be productive.

People who settled out here had to like the isolation. To him, Rachel had the right idea to choose life in a larger town. She'd have others around her besides her brother to keep her safe. Sure, she'd be better off in a fort. He didn't know if his particular role at Fort Dodge would allow for spouses, and a wife wasn't for him.

Lambert rode up to him. "Scout says the Stewarts are way ahead. He's only seen them once, and they moved on after that."

"Good to know, thank you. I hadn't even thought of them this afternoon," he replied. When the young man snickered, Patrick turned and glared at him. "Do you have something to say, soldier?"

"No, sir. I believe you."

"Good, because I don't believe me at all."

\*\*\*

"How far behind us do you suppose they are?"

Isaac shrugged while breaking a dry branch for the fire. "Not close but not far, either. I'd guess no more than five to seven miles."

Rachel nodded. The two of them were much faster. At any other time, she'd be thrilled to travel far each day. Today? Not so much when Captain Sinclair lagged further and further behind. If this afternoon was the last time she'd ever see him? She shook her head. There had to be a way for her to visit with him again.

"I reckon they'll overtake us and we'll do the same to them a few times before Santa Fe."

"Don't laugh, but I like staying around soldiers in case anything happens." She stirred a little more water into the flour. "Miss Ellie read stories to me from the newspaper about Indian attacks and buffalo stampedes."

"I heard some of those. She wanted you to stay with her."

"And you, too. She liked both of us."

Isaac flipped over the cooking ham with a fork. "Yeah, maybe. I'd like to think so." He nodded toward her as she made pan biscuits. "I'm glad you filled the pickle jar at Stranger's Creek."

She slapped a mosquito on her arm. "We should

have stopped there for the night. Can we put up muslin over the openings, or do you think the lack of breeze will be oppressive?"

"It's either sweat to death or be eaten up by bugs I guess."

"Looks like we'll have just enough for coffee tomorrow."

"I'll make sure we camp by water tomorrow night. I didn't plan ahead very well." He gave her a sly glance. "I'm used to men like Sinclair ordering me around when I travel." Isaac used the fork to point. "Go here, sit there, bunk here. Stand up, sit down, talk, don't talk."

She frowned at the surly tone in his voice. "Surely it's not as bad as all that."

"Maybe not. Some men needed the constant instruction. I didn't."

Rachel focused on setting the biscuits just so and avoided looking at him. Otherwise, she figured he'd see the skepticism in her face. Her brother hadn't trained to be a soldier before the war. He hadn't gone to strategy school or whatever troops did to learn how to march, shoot, and fight in general. Isaac had said officers went to West Point and had included Captain Sinclair in his statement.

Patrick would know what to do in any conflict. Senior officers had most likely given him their wisdom from prior conflicts. He'd escaped the Civil War unscathed, she thought, but reconsidered. Did anyone leave a battlefield unchanged? Isaac had been a happy-go-lucky fellow until he came home. She wondered what Patrick had been like before the war.

"Your biscuits are burning."

Rachel woke up out of her daydream. "Oh!" She moved fast to flip the four of them, only to find they all had black bottoms. "Phooey."

"Yep. If Ma were here, she'd laugh and make a joke about buttering, not burning, biscuits." He took the ham from the pan. "Meanwhile, I'm perfect."

"Your ham is perfect. Not you."

"I know better. In fact, I'll go put up the muslin while you redo our dinner. Just remember, we don't have all the flour in the world in our wagon. Try not to moon over Captain Wonderful while you're cooking."

Rachel laughed and threw one of the burnt biscuits at him, missing by a mile. She remixed a little more dough. Isaac was right. She could daydream about the captain after dinner.

By the time the food cooked, the sky glowed orange from the sunset. Isaac had finished up and wandered off without telling her where he was going. She hoped he'd be back soon. Rachel stood, stretching her legs. Smoke from the fire kept flies away. She bit her lip. Was answering nature's call worth scratching for the rest of the night?

"Is dinner ready? How's it looking?"

She glanced over at her brother. "Good. Still hot. Get started eating while I take a short walk."

"Sure."

He sat on one of the larger logs around the campfire. Rachel took care of her needs, glad they weren't the first to travel here. The lack of water must have made this an excellent place for a noonday meal. She liked the quiet. A stream would have meant more people around them tonight.

She stepped into the firelight and took a plate of

food from him. "Good?"

"Surprisingly, yes," he answered with his mouth full. He swallowed. "An open fire is different from a stove."

"Oh." Once seated, she took a bite of the ham. He was right. The food tasted just as good here as at home. "If we had a cow again, we'd have butter."

"Something to look forward to when we reach Santa Fe."

She nodded, eager to be rolling through New Mexico. "Right. I'd like a sewing shop in town, and civilization set up so close to the mountains means everything is perfect for farming."

"We'll have to live in a valley or get several oxen to pull a plow."

The farming tools sounded as expensive as the land would be. She'd need to write up new financial figures in her journal. "There are so many things we'll have to buy. I don't think we can own a farm this year or next."

"Probably not. I'll have to find work in town, too."

Rachel ate her last bite, not as optimistic as she'd been first thing in the morning. She didn't want to risk the trip only to go back to living in a one-room apartment with her brother. He was a good man, but she needed independence.

"You look worried. What's wrong?"

She didn't want to admit any dismay over repeating their life in Weston. "Nothing."

"Yes, there is, and I agree. I want my own place, too. Or at least my own bedroom. I want to start a family, work land I can leave to my children, start my life instead of always increasing someone else's wealth."

His words struck home with her. He'd voiced her wishes, too. Only, now when she considered settling down, Captain Sinclair was her husband. Rachel stared into the dying fire. He'd be in Kansas, and she'd be in New Mexico Territory. Her imagination would need a closer husband for her. Struggling to sound convincing, she said, "We'll both get what we want. I promise."

# CHAPTER SIX

Patrick stared out over the open plains. Hilly forests had given way to rolling and desolate hills. Now they all stood on a massive lump of stone called Pawnee Rock, rising up from the prairie. The country stretched out around them, beautiful in a wild and open way. He'd never seen so much sky all at once.

The view made killing rattlesnakes worth the effort. Gunshots cracked out every so often as his men found one hidden among the plum bushes or rocks. He'd read the names carved on the black sandstone and looked to see if Rachel's name was among them. Maybe the intermittent rattlers had distracted him from finding hers. Patrick crossed his arms against the cool, stiff breeze.

He'd traveled behind the Stewarts—he hoped. No signs of her or her brother lay along the road, something Patrick was both glad and sad to see. The past two weeks of missing her left him working hard to hide his irritation at life in general. He didn't want the last time they'd met to be the final time. Whenever he considered never seeing her again, his heart hurt.

"Did you look west?" Lambert asked him. "There might be a familiar wagon out there."

Patrick sighed. His second in command was the only person who knew his secret. "Yes. I've looked for her every hour of every day. I'm completely smitten. The only way I figure to get over her is to either find another woman or have her so close I get sick of her."

"What if neither way works?"

"Then, I don't know. Convince her Dodge is a great place, or figure a way to lead from Santa Fe."

Lambert clapped him on the back. "You'll figure it out, sir."

"Until then we'll camp here, but closer to the Arkansas."

The younger man nodded. "Will do. I'll tell the men."

He nodded and watched for a moment as Lambert picked his way to where the wagons and mules were waiting. The Arkansas River would be their companion until reaching their terminal fort. Patrick looked forward to seeing what sort of setup Fort Larned had. Fort Dodge was so new, and he expected the installation to be better.

From where he stood Patrick saw the first officer, Jenkins, and Rogers looking up at him. The men must be ready to make camp. He eased down the rocky hill while listening for rattlers along the way. Once at the bottom, he found his horse and followed the caravan to the river.

Later around the fire, beans and bacon bubbled in a pot. The various soldiers played cards. Patrick enjoyed the routine. Except, he wrote in his journal, he'd liked to have shared the day with Rachel. He glanced up from the page before ripping it out. The notes needed to be about the journey and not about impossible dreams. He tossed the wadded-up ball into the fire.

"Again?" Lambert asked.

"Mm-hm."

The trio of soldiers to his left stopped playing cards to look at him. One of them, Douglas, cleared his throat. "Sir, there are more women where she came from."

Instead of following his initial impulse to argue and say no lady could be Rachel's equal, Patrick stood. The sudden flush of anger from the offhand comment surprised him with its ferocity. He needed some time to cool down. Headed toward their supply wagon, he said over his shoulder, "Probably so. I'll write the day's notes after I get water for tomorrow's coffee."

He put his journal and pencil in his haversack and grabbed the coffeepot on his way to the river. The last little bit of daylight illuminated the trail to the water's edge. He enjoyed the warmth still rising from the heated ground. Cooled air from the water would wash over him every so often. The temperature reminded Patrick autumn would arrive soon. He walked between several large cottonwood trees, a movement on the opposite side catching his eye. An Indian woman was in the water with her toddler. He stopped cold, still as any statue.

No one else was near as they laughed and splashed in the river. The tribe must be nearby for the woman to be so carefree. She was a pretty gal, he figured, dressed in buckskins. Her black hair was braided on both sides. She didn't seem to mind getting the hem of her dress in the water. Considering how much the baby giggled while playing, Patrick wouldn't care either.

He watched as she played at bathing her son. The child reminded him of his nephew. All cheeks and a sunny disposition. If Josie and her family were here, she'd be just as full of fun with her son as this woman was with her baby. He missed his family and enjoyed watching the mother with her son.

She put the baby on the riverbank and began to undo her braids. Patrick panicked a little, figuring she was washing her own body next. Propriety demanded he alert her to his presence. He coughed and stepped forward to the water's edge. She turned in a whirl as if alarmed, before standing motionless. Even the baby stared at him with wide eyes. He nodded and knelt to fill the coffeepot. Once done, he turned and went back to camp.

The twilight gave him enough light to see by. He wondered if the mother and her child would be able to find their people in the semi-darkness. Josie would need a lantern for sure.

Similarities between the little family he'd just seen, and his own kept him preoccupied. Plus, he was still vastly irritated by Douglas implying Rachel was interchangeable with any other woman in the world. Patrick bypassed the group, letting them chatter amongst themselves, and set the coffee pot on the chuckwagon's tailgate.

"What's the matter, sir?" Lambert asked. "You look like you've seen a ghost."

Patrick turned toward him with a grin. "No—at least I hope they weren't." He shrugged. "Just a native woman with her child playing in the water."

"Too bad you didn't have your pistol," Rogers quipped. "Hit the woman first, then the child."

"Why not distract her by killing the child first?" another soldier offered.

"I reckon she'd be like any deer. You'd spook her, and she'd take off with it." Rogers shrugged. "No sense in missing both shots."

Patrick's fingernails dug into his palm. "This discussion is over. I would hope, as members of one of the finest armies in the world, we are better men than those who would kill innocent women and children."

An uncomfortable chuckle went through the group before Douglas said, "You're talking about them like they're people, sir."

He stared at each one of them as something in his mind clicked. All this time, the natives out west had been a primitive inconvenience keeping decent people from claiming and working the land. But after hearing Douglas' opinion, Patrick couldn't agree. They were the interlopers, pushing a population from their homeland. "They are as much a people as we are. We will not kill or injure women, children, or the elderly under any circumstances. Am I clear?"

"Yes, sir," several men from around the fire muttered.

"Excuse me, I don't think I heard any of you," Patrick said louder.

"Yes, sir!" they hollered.

"Much better. Cowards shoot at the unarmed, and not one of us is a coward." His anger fading to a dull roar, Patrick retrieved his journal and pencil.

"Consider what I've said as an order. Carry on."

He sat at the fire. The conversations gradually resumed their prior noise and bantering level. He stared at the blank journal page for several minutes. All he could think of was his soldiers executing the woman and her son in cold blood. He shivered and began to write the day's events.

# CHAPTER SEVEN

Isaac walked up to Rachel, his face as scowling as she felt. "So? What did the fort's blacksmith say?"

"We are not his first priority."

Rachel stomped her foot. "I wish I weren't a lady. He'd get a piece of my mind over the delay."

He walked past her and waited for her to fall in step with him before saying, "Understandable. I had a few choice words in my mind, too. Still, he's right. He has troops to keep rolling on their patrols west. We're not at the top of his list."

She let a soldier pass in front of them. "I know, but a week? I want to get there before the first snowfall."

"We weren't going to be there so soon even with perfect wheels."

"You're right." Rachel shook her head. "I suppose it could have been much worse. The wagon could have tipped, and we would have lost everything." They stepped off the boardwalk when it ended at the corner of a building. "I'll just have to adjust my plans."

"We've made good time so far," Isaac offered.

"Bossy's not sick. Neither one of us is, either. Remember the hotel in Cottonwood Falls? There have been some good things happen."

She nodded as they left the fort's perimeter for their campsite closer to the creek. "Our dinner there was the best. Too bad we didn't stay in the hotel." Rachel rushed in to add, "Saving money there means more to spend on our new home."

"That's the spirit." They reached their wagon. "I'd like to see who's riding up from Santa Fe. Ask about places hiring in or around town."

"Go ahead. I have some mending to do, plus I'd like to read a little bit while we're in one spot," she said. "I'll be safe enough here." Isaac gave her a mock salute and headed back to the fort.

Rachel shivered when a stiff wind rolled across the land. Every day they lingered meant camping out in a snowstorm. At least she had enough yarn for both of them to have new socks. She climbed up into the wagon and pulled her wooden trunk to the tailgate. Her knitting lay on top, over her journal and trail guide.

Half-done socks in hand, she sat on the edge of the tailgate and began knitting. The first awe over the vastness of Kansas had worn off by Pawnee Rock. Isaac had climbed to the top despite the snakes. She shuddered and missed a loop with her needle. He'd been insane to risk being bitten for a view. They'd have mountains and sunsets in New Mexico without the rattlers killing them.

She wondered how far Patrick was behind them now. Had he climbed Pawnee Rock, too, or did he have more sense and stayed safely on the ground? He seemed like such a sensible man to her. Not that Isaac was stupid, but avoiding venomous snakes was her deciding factor for intelligence.

Rachel paused to stretch out the sock. The cuff wasn't quite long enough for her brother. He liked socks up to his knees. Resuming, she wondered if the army gave Patrick his socks as a regular supply or if he needed to buy his own.

People traveling in the mountains would need warm gear. Hats, mittens, knitted gloves were all items she'd be able to make and sell. She smiled at the thought of owning her own needlework store. Who knew, she might send out bids to knit for the various forts in the area, maybe even including Fort Dodge. She'd have to measure, remeasure, and have him or any soldier try on her work lots of times.

"I don't think I've ever caught my mother or sister smiling while they knitted."

She glanced up in a hurry to find Patrick was standing in front of her. "Well, think of the devil, and he appears." She stood, putting her knitting on the tailgate. "I didn't even hear you walk up."

"We're trained to be stealthy, ma'am."

"I see." Her memory hadn't done him justice. The man gave the word handsome a new meaning. Even so, he seemed a little tired and a little thinner than a couple of weeks ago. "How are you and your soldiers?"

"Doing better." He leaned against the tailgate with her. "You know how it is when one person becomes sick and the rest follow."

"Were you ill, too?"

"Yep. I'll spare you the details except to say we all

regained our appetites."

"Oh." She tried not to imagine how horrible a group like theirs must have been with no one in good health. "We haven't had the same excitement. In fact, it's been rather mundane."

"Excluding our illness, we've been on the dull side, too. I'm not complaining, though." He stared at her work for a couple of minutes before adding, "My day has become a lot more exciting in the past few moments."

Rachel paused and looked at him. His eyes twinkled, their warm brown also warming her heart. "Be careful what you wish for concerning excitement, Captain Sinclair. I'm sure there are natives out there who'd love to liven up your journey with an arrow or two."

He laughed and nudged her with his shoulder. "I'm sure there are, but as long as you're safe, I'll be fine."

She leaned closer to him with a grin. "You're such a sweet talker."

"Only to you."

Isaac walked up to them before she could reply. "I can't leave you alone without some mangy ol' soldier trying to court you, can I?"

Patrick's eyebrows rose. "Excuse me? Mangy?"

He laughed, moving to shake Patrick's hand. "A little around the edges, sir. How are you?"

Taking his hand, Patrick grinned. "Doing well. Lagging behind our schedule, but it's to be expected. I came over to tell Miss Stewart about rumors concerning Fort Dodge. Sounds to me like they need people to work there."

Isaac grinned. "So does everyone. The war set back

a lot of people and their families. I don't mind making a living helping others."

Rachel put her knitting back in the trunk while asking, "What led you to decide on the dry route to Dodge?"

"We have water containers, and I wanted to make up for lost time."

She shook her head. "Our pickle jar wasn't enough for the three of us."

"Bossy's a heavy drinker," Isaac interjected.

"As are you," Rachel teased. "But when our wheel began falling apart, we had to backtrack and come here."

Patrick frowned. "And that's been how long?"

"Four days."

His frown deepened, and he crossed his arms. "Are you having one built from scratch?"

She looked at Isaac to explain. "No, the outside metal band began splitting and broke apart as we rolled up to the fort."

Her brother continued, "The blacksmith said it's a simple fix he doesn't have time to do."

"I see. Has he given you an estimate on how long it will take?"

Isaac shrugged. "He said he can't commit to anything."

"All right." He glanced at the row of stores before turning back to her. "I have an errand. Would you two care to have supper with us this evening? We have plenty, more than we need."

"I'd like that, yes." Ignoring her stomach's flutter of excitement, she turned to her brother. "Isaac?"

He shrugged. "Why not?"

"Good." Patrick grinned from ear to ear. "I'll be back in a moment."

She watched him walk away and toward the fort. Something about him left her heart racing and her knees weak.

Isaac leaned over to her. "He's just making up an excuse to spend the evening with you."

"I don't mind. He can use any reason he'd like to see me again."

He groaned. "Excuse me while I go retch from all this sweetness you're dishing out to the rest of us."

"Retch away, dear brother." She laughed at his resulting sick expression and hopped up to sit on their wagon's tailgate. "Meanwhile, I'll finish the cuff on your sock." Rachel resumed her work and listened to Isaac gossip about various people at the fort. She knew a few of the people he referenced. Getting out and making friends was good for him. She'd worried about his isolation and figured he needed more people around him than just her.

"Looks like your puppy dog is back."

"Hmm?" She didn't recall any dogs and glanced up to see Patrick approaching them. "Be nice." After he sighed, she smacked his leg. "Seriously. He's a good man."

"The smithy says your wheel will be ready as soon as the new metal cools. You'll be able to leave tomorrow morning when we do." He looked at Isaac. "Will you need help?"

"Rachel and I removed the broken wheel. We can reattach the fixed one."

Patrick's lips thinned. "A couple of my men will be over to help you as soon as the wheel's ready."

Isaac's eyes narrowed. "That's not necessary. She and I did the job just fine without you and your soldiers. We'll also be good once you leave."

The captain's chin lifted as if struck. Rachel gripped the sock in her hand. She'd faced angry customers while at Miss Ellie's. But now? She didn't want to be the cause of anyone's fuss. "Please don't bother sending anyone over, Captain." She hopped up, putting the sock behind her. "You've done more than enough to help us."

His stern expression softened when he looked at her. "I promise it's no bother for my men to help a fine lady like you."

Crossing his arms, Isaac added, "And it helps your ulterior motive."

Patrick stared at the other man for a few seconds. "You're right. I do have an ulterior motive concerning you and your sister. We're going in the same direction. There's two of you, a contingent of us, and hostiles lined up between here and there. My goal is to keep you safe. Even if it's against your will."

He turned on his heel and left with Rachel staring after him. Isaac spit on the ground. "Uppity, isn't he? His type is all the same, ordering us around like we can't fend for ourselves."

Rachel bit her lip to keep from arguing with her mercurial brother. Patrick's concern warmed her heart. Even if his care was only because of duty, she liked his consideration for their well-being. "I'd still like to have dinner with him and the soldiers. I'm tired of my own cooking."

"Of course, we'll go. A free meal is a free meal." He nodded toward the fort. "Would you look at that.

Being an officer does have its privileges."

She watched as a couple of soldiers, younger than her, rolled their wagon wheel over to them. "I'll say. Don't start complaining, because this really is a favor Captain Sinclair didn't have to do."

Isaac just grumbled under his breath as they approached. Rachel wanted to get out of having to help and be the refined lady Patrick said she was. "I'd like to clean up before we eat."

"So go," he replied as the men came up.

Rachel nodded a greeting and hurried to her trunk to take out her favorite soap. On a whim, she grabbed a small blanket and set out her Sunday dress. She'd like to be pretty for dinner no matter what day it happened to be.

As soon as she hopped down, the men began their work. She went to the Pawnee River and placed the small blanket and soap on the bank. After kicking off her shoes, she picked her way through the brush to the water. Rachel made a mental note to make new clothes for herself and Isaac.

Her best dress was a little old. The hem didn't entirely cover her ankles. The cloth also hung from her slender frame since she'd been heavier before the war. Still, the cream color brought out the blue of her eyes and the golden parts of her hair.

She debated on not washing her hair before deciding to go ahead. This close to the fort meant she'd have to bathe while dressed. Rachel didn't mind. She'd not had a decent bath since Weston. Santa Fe and a large tub of warmish water would be heavenly. She daydreamed about getting clean in her own bedroom while scrubbing her scalp with the rose-scented soap.

Rachel rinsed the suds from her hair and face in the now-muddy water. The river didn't flow enough to provide clear water, another reason to not like settling around Fort Larned. The prairie might be vast and beautiful, but she dreamed of blue mountains and green valleys in a land of warm sunshine.

Her hair and face squeaky clean, Rachel climbed the bank and grabbed her shoes to carry. She wrapped the small blanket around her hair before setting off toward the wagon. The wet dress clung to her, so she crossed her arms. No one else was around her as she hurried to their camp. The new wheel was in place and her brother gone, so she climbed up into the wagon with some effort. "Darn skirts," she muttered.

Rachel pulled up the tailgate and closed the holes in the canvas. Soon, she wore her best clothes and had her work dress hung over the seat to dry. She took down the covers to let the breeze keep the wagon cooler. She let down the tailgate and sat to comb her hair with her mother's silver comb. The strands only went to a little way below her shoulders. Before the war, she'd let her hair go to her waist. She sighed. Maybe one day when she had the time to care for long hair, she'd stop trimming her locks.

Rachel glanced up to see Patrick staring at her. She stopped combing in mid-movement. He wore a hungry expression she'd felt when seeing him nearby. Patrick took a couple of steps forward. "I hope I'm not disturbing you."

"You're not. Not at all." She finished her combing and smiled. "I thought I'd dress for dinner since it's been so long since I've had an invitation."

The hungry look never left his face. "You always have an invitation, Rachel. Whenever, wherever, however, you desire."

Her heart thudded in her chest. He stared at her in the same way she felt for him. "The same goes for you, too. You're welcome anywhere at any time."

His gaze swept from her damp and curling hair to her bare feet. He smiled when seeing her toes. "I'm glad to hear that. I suppose the men fixed your wheel, or you'd be sitting sideways by now."

She chuckled. "Yes, they did. Thank you for your help."

"My pleasure." He tipped his hat. "I look forward to your company tonight."

"I look forward to yours as well."

He grinned before going to the fixed wheel. Seemingly satisfied, he tipped his hat again and went back to the fort.

She watched as he walked away. His appearance always caught her eye. The man was handsome and everything she'd ever wanted in a husband. He'd make any woman look twice, and she loved how he cared for her and even tolerated Isaac.

Her brother might complain, but it was nice to have extra help after so long with merely her and her mother. She'd spent several months alone before Isaac had come home from the war. Having the room above the shop had been nice, but lonely. Patrick disappeared among the crowd of soldiers milling around, and she missed him already. She might not need Patrick, but she certainly wanted him.

While she combed and daydreamed, Isaac walked up to their wagon, talking with a friend he'd made. The man saw her and stopped mid-sentence with his mouth hanging open. Her brother turned to her and frowned. "Your good dress for a campfire meal? Where do you think you are?"

"I think I'm in the middle of the wilderness and waiting for my working dress to dry." She hopped off of the tailgate, bare feet on the ground. "You might be a little friendlier with bathing yourself."

As the other man laughed, he shrugged and said, "Sure, maybe later."

Rachel frowned as he walked off. Really, his sour attitude irritated her sometimes. Their wheel was fixed, they'd have a military escort tomorrow, and a free dinner tonight. The way she saw it, Isaac had no reason to complain. She searched for and found the knitting. If she worked hard, she'd have this sock finished before dinner.

Later, she turned her head side to side to loosen the kinks in her neck. The sun hovered above the horizon, and the air was rich with burnt meat aromas. Her stomach growled, and she set aside her knitting. Isaac was God knows where and she was hungry. Even better, any of Patrick's men had to be better cooks over a campfire than she was.

Rachel slipped into her shoes. Patrick's men camped out like they did so they couldn't be in the fort proper. She wandered along the perimeter of Fort Larned to look for them. Her face warmed when realizing she'd stared at the captain to the exclusion of everything else whenever they met. So much so that she couldn't remember anything about his men.

At last, she found him. Patrick stood with a group of seemingly important men near a campfire. She recognized some of the soldiers sitting nearby and paused. What if he were busy discussing important issues and she intruded? Rachel reached for her apron. She'd worn the cover to protect her good dress.

"Miss Stewart." Patrick broke away from his group and walked up to her. "Dinner is almost ready." He glanced around. "Will your brother be joining us?"

"Maybe. I'm not sure."

He looked in her wagon's direction. "I see. Anyway, please have a seat and you'll be served first."

She did as he suggested, sitting by a young soldier who looked twelve years old. Rachel nodded at him as he stirred the food. "Hello."

"Hello, ma'am."

Not quite sure what to say next Rachel sat there, watching everyone. Patrick was the tallest and had the broadest shoulders. His uniform seemed cleaner, and he smiled much more often than anyone else.

"So, ma'am, when are you and the captain getting married?"

She stared at the cook with her heart in her throat. "Married? I, um, we haven't discussed anything."

"Oh."

He continued on without comment. Rachel glanced at Patrick, who was close enough to have heard if he were paying attention. Judging from his bright red face, he had listened to the question. She smiled at the cooking soldier. "I'm sure when the time is right, Captain Sinclair will declare his intentions to any woman lucky enough to have captured his attention. Until then, the rest of us will have to simply make do with waiting."

She watched him during her reply, and he looked

away from her at the end. Rachel glanced around for Isaac, spotting him walking over to the group. He wouldn't be pleased about the marriage question. To divert the conversation from her to anyone else, she asked, "Were you in the war?"

"Yes, ma'am. The last little bit of it. I helped General Sherman go through Georgia and stop the Rebs."

He went on about his experiences and Rachel listened with only half an ear. She couldn't pay full attention when Patrick stood so nearby. Her brother was with the captain and his men as they talked before all of them settled in around her.

Patrick sat on her right and Isaac on her left. Both men were engrossed in reliving past battles. Rachel would prefer to forget the Civil War ever happened and focus on the future. Others obviously disagreed. The young soldier gave her a plate of meat and potatoes, some of the best she'd ever eaten.

The men around her ate and talked as if she wasn't there. Patrick gave her a glance every so often, and his cook made sure she had plenty to eat. Otherwise, they left her alone. She didn't like being ignored but did enjoy listening to the stories and laughter. Even Isaac seemed to have a good time.

Patrick smiled at her. "Do you want an extra escort back to your camp?"

"Besides you?" she asked, forgetting about her brother for a moment. "Oh, I mean, yes, if you're offering."

"I am."

"No," Isaac interrupted. "She's safe with me. You have more important things to do than hover over civilians who don't need your help."

One of Patrick's eyebrows rose, and Rachel turned to her brother. "Him walking us to our wagon won't hurt anything."

"No, he's right," Patrick said. "You two are fine on your own. We'll meet up tomorrow morning anyway."

"Very well, until tomorrow," she replied and walked backward until Patrick was out of sight. Isaac had gone on ahead. She hurried to catch up with him. "Why are you being so rude?"

"You need to remember what those animals did to our farm." He grabbed her upper arm and squeezed until Rachel yelped. He shook her. "They burned everything. Killed our livestock and destroyed or stole our crops. Union soldiers broke our father and killed our mother."

She wrenched her arm from his grip with a wince. "They're not all bad. You forget your own time as a Union soldier and Pa's time as well."

"I heard what the kid asked you about Sinclair." He followed as she led the way to their wagon. "Letting him help us is one thing, but marrying one of those bastards is unacceptable."

With her back to him, she said, "I'm never marrying a soldier because living with you has been trying enough." Rachel let down the tailgate with a thud. "You'll need to calm down and understand I'm not marrying anyone."

She kicked off her shoes. "Besides, Union soldiers can't be trusted to do the right thing in any circumstances unless they're you or our father. I couldn't marry a man I can't trust." Rachel glanced at Isaac to see why he was so quiet. Judging by how he stared behind her, she guessed turning around might be a bad idea.

"Miss Stewart, you dropped this before you left our camp."

Rachel felt the empty space in her apron pocket and winced. She forced herself to face Patrick. Sure enough, he held the envelope from Miss Ellie. "I see. Thank you for returning it to me." She took the money from him.

"Count it."

"I'm sure it's all there." A metallic taste of fear lingered at the back of her throat. He had an air of quiet fury around him. She gulped. "I trust you."

"Count it. Every bill," he growled. "I'm not leaving until you do."

# CHAPTER EIGHT

The early morning rustle of the fort waking up stirred Patrick from his sleep. Groggy from a rare good, if unexciting, dream, he rubbed his eyes and sat up. Anger-tinged sadness settled over him like the fog blanketing the dewy grass. Isaac's comments last night irritated him, but Rachel's responses had hurt.

He sat up, the straw tick mattress thin under him. A bed beat the ground every time. He began rolling up his bedding before dressing. While he straightened up his area, he grinned. Isaac's eyes had grown bigger and bigger as Rachel counted. He hadn't known about the money, apparently, and Patrick would have loved to have been there for the conversation about her deception.

Still, his heart hurt over her thinking he'd steal from anyone, never mind her. Patrick stepped out of the room while the other officers slept. He'd adored Rachel when she sewed for him and more so every time they met. But now? He fastened the last button at the top of his shirt. He still cared for her, but with feelings far more guarded than before her comments.

Lambert snapped to attention as he approached. "Good morning, sir. We're finishing breakfast and will be ready to go whenever you say."

His stomach growled. "Save any for me?"

He glanced back at Jenkins, who nodded. Patrick grinned as the cook dished him up a plate. "Thank you. I like Rogers' cooking better than any mess hall."

"Good deal, sir. I might not mention your preference to Molly. She'll come out here to tan your hide personally."

Patrick chuckled and settled in with his food. He didn't waste any time eating. "Are the Stewarts ready to go?"

The two men exchanged glances before Lambert said, "We haven't seen either of them this morning."

Patrick nodded. They might still be asleep or even gone. Slinking away from embarrassment would be the coward's way to go. While he didn't think either Stewart would choose to run and hide, after last night's accusations he wouldn't bet on anything with those two. "Very well. I'll check on them myself."

Jenkins took his plate before Patrick walked away. The newer buildings of Fort Larned glistened in the sunrise. He breathed in deep and enjoyed the crisp air. He'd be happy if Fort Dodge was even half as good as Larned.

The siblings' wagon lay ahead with no signs of activity. Even the fire was out. As he approached he said, "Mr. Stewart? Miss Stewart? Anyone here?" He walked up to find the horse gone, too. Irritated at the lack of response, he peered into the wagon bed. "Hello?"

Rachel was alone and snuggled in a quilt. She stirred in her sleep with a little snort and his anger melted away. Most of it did, anyway. He still frowned at her harsh words, but looking at her now healed some of the hurt. She smiled while dreaming. He wondered how someone so beautiful could be so mean. He'd never given her one reason to doubt his word and an officer's word was his bond. Patrick cleared his throat. "Miss Stewart, time to wake up."

She opened her eyes and sat up with a start. Clutching the quilt to her, she looked around with a groggy expression. "Hmm? Where's Isaac?"

"I have no idea. I'm not your brother's keeper," he said, and she flinched. He ignored the urge to apologize for being rude. "We're almost ready to go. If you're still interested in our protection to Fort Dodge, I'd suggest you wake up and find Mr. Stewart."

"Mm-hmm, I will," she replied as he turned on his heel and walked away.

She didn't trust him. He had to remember her feelings and not give in to his. All Patrick wanted to do was crawl into her wagon and hold her until she woke up completely. He shivered, wishing he'd paused long enough to put on his jacket. Otherwise, he'd not need to cuddle her under a warm blanket for the rest of the morning.

Patrick shook his head as if to shake off the desire. Both she and her bitter wretch of a brother were best forgotten the instant they reached Fort Dodge. His irritation went with him to his camp. The men all looked at him but didn't say a word. They'd taken his statement about appropriate topics to discuss seriously last night. "They'll either be ready soon, or we'll leave them behind. Now, is Douglas caring for the stock? I assume he is?"

"Yes, sir," Jenkins replied while putting out the campfire. "He left right after you did to round up the oxen."

"Good. Let's get going."

\*\*\*

Rachel's stomach churned. Patrick was furious, and she couldn't blame him at all. She'd said ugly things to Isaac about him last night. Things meant to calm and reassure him, not for Patrick to ever hear.

She sighed and crawled out from under her quilt. Time to find Isaac and Bossy, so they weren't left behind. She put up covers and changed into her everyday dress. By the time she was tying on her apron, she heard what she hoped was her brother and their horse outside.

She peeked out before letting down the tailgate. Her brother stood there, frowning. Rachel hopped to the ground. "Captain Sinclair was here. They're leaving soon. Are we ready?"

"Not very, but yes. I'll hitch up Bossy if you make sure everything else is picked up."

Rachel nodded and rushed around to clean up the area. The lack of coffee disappointed her. Isaac had time to wander around but not fix any for either of them? She'd need to roast beans for chewing on when water was scarce.

Tonight. She'd roast tonight. They didn't have time for anything at the moment, and Patrick hadn't mentioned which route they'd be taking, wet or dry. One way, they'd follow the Arkansas River. The other, they'd be riding over barren land.

Rachel grabbed their coffee pot and pickle jar before heading for the Pawnee. She wandered upstream a little way for the clearest water. Just as her jar finished filling, a low whistle rolled over the prairie to her. She hurried across to their wagon to find Isaac already seated. He barely waited until she was inside before starting off.

She secured the water and climbed her way to the front to sit. They rolled on for a few miles without talking. She glanced over at him. He seemed a lot more awake than she felt at the moment. But then the fuss yesterday hadn't gnawed at him like it had her.

"Looks like we're going the dry route," Isaac said.

Rachel nodded and reached behind for her guidebook. "I wondered if we might."

"We'll need to think of Bossy."

"I filled the pickle jar for her."

"And the coffee?" Isaac asked. "I saw you carried it, too."

"Yes, that too." She thumbed through her guide and stopped on the part about finding water. The smooth road let her read while moving. Rachel finished the chapter and reread the part about fixing broken wagon wheels by the time the group stopped at noon.

She looked all around as if waking up from a dream. Like the guide suggested, they had advance and rear guards. Soldiers kept a watch over the group. They'd trade off, she noticed, but never found Captain Sinclair among them.

Isaac followed the others and eased their wagon to a stop. "I don't think we have time for cooking."

"Probably not." She crept back into the wagon

while he unhooked a wash pan. "We didn't eat the dinner I had planned for last night, so it can be a lunch today."

"Let me guess, biscuits?"

"Smart man! Yes."

His face appeared at the wagon's back opening, and he grabbed the pickle jar. "At least you're getting better at cooking them."

"And throwing them when you sass me."

He gave her a rare smile before disappearing to provide Bossy a drink. Rachel unwrapped the food. The biscuits were dry, but then so was everything out here. She put away the extra before bringing the bread and several dried apple slices up front.

Isaac glanced up at her. "Do you want a drink before I put back the water?"

"Yes, please."

He drank first, leaving more than plenty for her. After she had her fill, she gave the half-empty jar back to him. "Thank you. Your lunch is ready when you are."

A whistle sounded, and he said, "I guess I'm ready now." He rushed to put away the pan and jar. He rejoined her just in time to begin rolling with the troops. They ate, and when he'd swallowed his last bite Isaac said, "When were you going to tell me about the money?"

"Later, when we were closer to Santa Fe."

"So, you trust me as much as you do that captain, hmm?"

"I trust both of you," she began, and his scoff interrupted her for a moment. "I do, and you know it. I just liked having the money on me."

"Oh, I'm sure. You liked having all the money and keeping it for yourself."

"I was going to share with you."

"When? At Santa Fe? We could have used the money at Larned for our wheel." He glared at her. "Or did you plan on running off with Captain Pretty Pants, leaving me alone in New Mexico?"

Her mouth dropped open, and if she weren't so enraged, she'd laugh at his mocking of Patrick. "You don't know what it was like during the war. The farm was gone. Do you know what that means? Ma and I were on the streets, and if not for Miss Ellie taking us in I'd have been there when you came back."

She shook her head before he could rebut. "No, let me tell you how horrible it was for us. We had to camp out along the river for weeks before finding Miss Ellie." Rachel waved her arms at the wagon. "All this we have now is luxury compared to what we had along the Missouri River. Miss Ellie gave us a home even after Ma became ill. She could have turned us out, afraid of getting sick herself."

Rachel blinked away the tears and wiped her cheeks. "I know the war was hell for you and Pa, and I'm sorry. But we suffered, too." She ignored memories of holding her mother's hand until her fingers grew cold. "I just wanted the satisfaction of having some sort of means to care for myself, is all. I wanted a little bit of security of my own."

She sniffed and looked at him. "You have to know I would always share what I have with you. This time, I just wanted to feel safe."

He put his arm around her and held her close while she sobbed. When she quieted, he said, "I'm sorry, truly I am, and I do understand. Our world was quicksand for too long. I need to realize I'm not the only one still feeling the effects."

She let him hold her for a while as they rolled onward. Soon, she stopped sniffling and sat upright. "I suppose I could read a little of the guidebook. See what sort of emergencies we might encounter."

"Might as well. The road here is a lot smoother than I'd expected."

Rachel smiled and fished her book out of her apron pocket. Every time she reread a chapter, she'd learned something missed in a time or two before. She kept one eye out for Patrick but never saw him. Her heart ached over the expression on his face this morning. He'd alternated between his usual affectionate look and a newly formed, irritated one.

"I don't know why you care about the man," Isaac offered. "After Fort Dodge, you'll probably never see him again. Focus on Santa Fe, because that's where our future lies. Not with some wandering army captain."

She hated how he always seemed to know her thoughts. Rachel nodded and stared out at the flat land around them. The harsh wind was constant. She let it be the excuse to not answer back. The truth was, she didn't want to argue with him about anything concerning Patrick. The loss of his friendship was too new a wound.

The day wore on until, at last, they stopped at a rare clump of trees. The wind blew strong still. She hopped down from the seat, her legs stiff from inactivity.

"Ma'am?"

One of the younger soldiers stood at her side.

Rachel smiled at him. "Yes?"

"Captain Sinclair wanted me to let you know there will be no campfires until after dark."

She glanced at Isaac, who nodded. "Of course. We'll wait until then."

"Thank you, ma'am." He tipped his hat and continued on to the next wagon.

Rachel helped Isaac unhitch Bossy. She said, "You gave in pretty easily."

"Burning down our only home just to spite some army captain won't get us anywhere."

"I agree." Watching as he poured the last from the pickle jar for their horse, Rachel bit her lip. "The guidebook mentioned digging for water. I might see if the trees are growing around an oasis of sorts."

"Sure. Couldn't hurt to find out. You might keep an eye open for firewood."

"I will." She grabbed a small shovel from the sideboard and headed for the copse. The shade refreshed her. Not until she was under the canopy did she realize how hot the late afternoon had been. Enjoying the pocket of cool air, she watched for sandy soil to dig.

"Do you need some privacy?"

She glanced up to see Patrick up ahead of her, a sly grin on his face. "What?" He nodded at her shovel and her face burned. "Oh, no, I don't. Not now." His eyebrows rose as if he didn't believe her. "It's true. I'm looking for a marshy place to dig. Our water jar is empty, and I don't want to drink up what's supposed to be coffee in the morning."

"We have plenty of water in barrels. There's no need for you two to go without." He walked up closer.

"And besides, digging around for water is Isaac's responsibility, isn't it? Why did he send you out to do a man's job?"

Rachel let him take the shovel. "I decided to come out here on my own." She followed him and looked at the ground, too. "He was taking care of our horse and setting up for the night. I usually help but without a campfire, there's not much to do."

His assumption of her business with the shovel stopped her. "Oh, goodness. I'm not keeping you from *your* necessary privacy, am I? I can leave and let you be alone."

He chuckled. "No, I'm fine. Out here scouting the area. After the past few days, I find I'm a little homesick for forests."

She snorted a laugh. "In that case, I'd suggest you pull up some saplings from around here. If Fort Dodge is anything like what we've seen so far, you'd be better off building a grove of stacked buffalo chips." She smiled at his laugh. "You'll have smelly sod trees."

"I prefer saplings, now that you mention it." He stopped and turned to her. "I don't think the water is close enough to the surface for what you want. There's a thin line of sand I could try."

"Or I could. I don't mind."

He shook his head. "No, I'll do it." Patrick knelt and used the short shovel to dig in the soft soil.

She watched as he went down a foot before finding any moisture. "The book made it sound as if water would rush in for me."

"It's been dry this year. I suppose to make up for the excessive rainfall last year." He paused. "Seriously, we do have plenty for you and yours. Part of us protecting you is providing supplies when necessary."

She stared down at Patrick and resisted the urge to hold him close. The affection he had for her shown clearly on his face as he stood upright. "If you're sure you don't mind?"

"Not at all." He examined her face for a moment and brushed a stray lock from her forehead. "I'd better fill this back up, so no one stumbles in the middle of the night."

"Or I can if you have more important things to do."

"I won't say I don't." He paused to wink at her before kneeling again and going back to work. "But I would rather be in the woods with a pretty girl than ordering around anyone else."

Rachel watched him. She needed to clear the air between them so this awful uneasiness would disappear. "So, concerning last night and what I said…"

The covering done, he stood to face her. "Our main cook at Fort Leavenworth mentioned General Order Number Eleven. Your family had lost a lot to Union soldiers. I can understand your bitterness."

"Thank you, but those soldiers weren't you." She crossed her arms. "I'd like to think you'd be the calm voice in that storm."

"I'd like to think so, too, but war is a horrible thing. You don't know until you're in the middle of a battle."

She took the shovel he offered. "Looting and burning our homes wasn't a battle."

"No, I don't suppose it was." He shook his head. "I don't have a reason for what they did. I'm not sure if the measures helped stop the fighting in Missouri and Kansas. All I can do is help you and Isaac as some sort of reparation for what you've lost."

"It's not your responsibility."

"Maybe not, but helping you would be my pleasure." He took a few steps toward camp. "Let's go fill your water jar from our stores."

"All right." She glanced around to make sure they were alone and took hold of his arm. "Captain Sinclair, um, Patrick? I still need to apologize and explain myself."

"I see no need for you to do anything of the sort."

"No, I do." Rachel took a deep breath and looked him in the eyes. "I said those things about trusting you to mollify my brother and steady my runaway feelings." She swallowed when his frown deepened. "I truly do trust you." She clasped her hands and steeled herself to continue. "I also care for you far more than I should. You've been nothing but brave and kind to me, us, since our first encounter, and I'm loathe to leave you behind when we continue on to Santa Fe."

He squinted. "You're not playing a game?"

"No. I'm being honest."

"Why didn't you tell your brother about the money?"

Her heart pounded in her throat as he stared at her for several long seconds. "I wanted to enjoy having it. We'd gone without for so long. I just wanted the security of money in my pocket."

"You're lucky you didn't lose it anywhere else but next to me."

"I agree. If I had to lose funds like I did, I can't imagine doing so next to a better man than you.

You're a fine example of everything a good person should be." She tilted her head and gave him a wry grin. "Although, if all Union soldiers were like you, I'd still have a farm and we'd have never met."

"I don't know whether to curse or thank them. I'd love to wring their necks for hurting you, but my life would be empty without you in it."

"You have feelings for me?"

I think it's obvious I do." He leaned forward, so close their lips almost touched. "I care for you so very much."

# CHAPTER NINE

Patrick caught himself. He pulled away before their lips touched. "Pardon me—I've forgotten my manners."

Her eyes opened wide. "Oh! I have, too." She put a hand over her mouth. "You are rather bewitching, Captain Sinclair."

He grinned. "Funny, considering I think I'm the one under a spell."

"We should rejoin the others."

"Why? You're not afraid of me, are you?"

Rachel caressed his face for a few seconds before replying. "No, I'm afraid of me."

His body tensed as desire coiled throughout him. "In that case, we do need to find the others." He resisted adding anything else and instead led her back to the main group. "I'll walk you back to your wagon."

"Thank you. I've often wondered something. When a soldier is assigned someplace, how long does he usually stay?"

Patrick considered her question. Did she mean his

orders in particular, or was she merely making conversation? He took a chance and answered, "The time varies based on what the needs are. In my case, I'll be at Dodge for two years unless extended another two."

"You could stay as long as four years?" She shook her head. "The time seems so long. What if you found a reason to move before then? Would you?"

"I'd have to ask my commanding officer first. To find out if a position is open." He glanced at her, his heart thudding in his chest. "The closest fort to Santa Fe is Union." Patrick nodded toward his wagon. "The locations are a few days apart. Come on. I have a map to show you."

She followed along for a few steps before he stopped and reached for the shovel. "Let me carry that for you."

After a chuckle, she said, "Here, you can be a gentleman. It isn't heavy, though."

"The weight doesn't matter. I want the chance to be mannerly." He tilted his head. "Especially while I can be."

"Very well," she murmured and went with him when he continued.

He ignored the stares from his men as they approached the wagons. The wind had died enough to let various campfires start. He noticed the Stewart wagon had its own fire.

Rachel should probably be at her camp and cooking, but Patrick didn't care. He had her attention and wanted to keep it for as long as possible. After letting down the tailgate, he retrieved his logbook. "I use this to keep papers and a journal." He flipped through the pages to find the latest survey of Kansas. "Here. We're right here."

She stared at the illustration. "My book doesn't have maps."

"What are you using?"

"This guidebook." She went to retrieve a book from her apron pocket and gave it to him. "Here. *The Prairie and Overland Traveler.*"

He smiled, surprised she kept the book with her all the time. Patrick gave her his book and opened her volume with its dark red cover to read the title page. "1860? We've done a little bit of land surveying since then."

She grinned at him while flipping through his journal. "I suppose so."

"Our maps are updated once a year at least," he said while scanning the table of contents. "There are constant changes."

"Should I be reading your notes? Or are they for government eyes only?"

Patrick shrugged, engrossed by her book's description of a *Journada del Muerto* along the Santa Fe Trail. "You can read anything you like. I don't write classified information in my personal journal."

"Personal?"

"Somewhat, yes. Too much so for the army, but not so much to make you blush." He glanced up to see her cheeks were redder than usual. "Oops. Too late." Patrick went back to find out where this *Muerto* was and if she'd be going along the route. "You might see a mention of me meeting a charming young woman who let me into her shop after closing hours. Nothing else is as private."

He glanced over, to find her cheeks glowed. Beyond her, Isaac approached. "I think your brother needs you to cook dinner."

She turned and sighed. "I'm afraid so." Rachel gave him back his book and took hers. "Thank you for a lovely time."

"You won't want to have dinner with us? The food must be good because no one's interrupted our conversation yet." At her quizzical expression, he added, "They're keeping everything for themselves."

She chuckled. "Smart of them. Sadly, no. I have to get back to our own camp." Isaac stood by her as she added, "We're out of biscuits for tomorrow, and I still need to find water for Bossy."

"You've reminded me." He whistled. "Rogers, Douglas, come here." The two soldiers came around the corner. "The Stewarts need one of our smaller water barrels."

"We don't," Isaac protested.

He motioned at his stationary men, and they took off. While giving a glare at her brother, Patrick said, "Everyone needs water, and we're on the dry route. Don't drink any, if you're so inclined, but don't deprive your sister or animal."

Isaac crossed his arms. "All right. Rachel? Are you expecting me to cook tonight?"

"No. More like hoping," she replied before addressing Patrick. "Thank you and your men for the help. Goodnight."

"Sleep well," he replied. Isaac gave him a final frown before falling into step behind her. The man's bad attitude irritated but didn't anger him like his stubborn neglect of Rachel. The two soldiers went by him, carrying the full barrel. "Thank you, men."

They gave their "Welcome, sir's" as he headed for the campfire. Whatever Jenkins was cooking left his stomach rumbling. He put the journal back in with his other belongings and headed for their fire. He nodded a greeting to the few men gathered and noticed his first officer wasn't there. Patrick considered it a blessing at the moment.

He sat on a wooden box, one of the few free. Every evening was the same. Drive across the country, settle down, eat, write, and sleep until the morning. He took a cup of stew offered after making sure the others had their own meal. A piece of cornbread sat on top. Patrick glanced around. None of the men seemed to have a problem with the bread. Not like he did.

Repressing the urge to toss the piece as far as he could throw, he pushed the bread aside and ate the stew. No one else knew of his time at the Confederates' Cahaba prison. He wanted to keep his ordeal a secret. Patrick never spoke of what had happened there. He didn't write it in letters home or in his journal. His family in Ohio already knew. He had no reason to remind them.

As awful as the prison was, Cahaba had been a resort stay compared to what others went through at Andersonville. He knew to be grateful. Still, getting rid of the fleas had been difficult and deeply humiliating. Other prisoners resembled walking skeletons while he waited with them in the parole camp at Vicksburg. So many of them had died in a steamship's explosion. He glanced up at the late evening sky and the first stars twinkling. Every day was a gift.

Patrick mashed around the bread in the last few

teaspoons of broth. The South at the end of the war had barely enough food and clothing for their soldiers. Prisoners received nearly nothing. Between disease, starvation, and insect infestations, some of the wounded never stood a chance at survival. They'd had no way to cook the ingredients given them while incarcerated in the converted warehouse.

He'd die and go to hell before he'd eat cornmeal or rodent ever again.

"Sir?" Rogers sat down beside him. "We delivered the water. Did you want us to send another barrel tomorrow?"

"No."

\*\*\*

Rachel opened her eyes. Isaac slept nearby, his snores having woken her. She smiled as the last thing on her mind before sleeping returned to her thoughts. Patrick had written, "Must return to Weston ASAP" on the evening they'd met. Reading in his journal a couple of days ago about how he'd shared her affections from the beginning continued to make her happy.

She sighed and sat up. They'd been so close to kissing. She could almost still feel his breath on her lips. Clove, she suspected while creeping out of the wagon bed. He always managed to smell spicy. She'd have to ask him why cinnamon one day, mint the next, and clove the day after.

Nature was calling her, thanks to plenty of water Patrick's men had provided them. She eased out of the wagon. The entire camp lay quiet. Fires had died down to embers, which gave her a little bit of light to see a couple of the men guarding them. Very few trees or bushes grew around them. She went to one of the guards and whispered, "I need to take a necessary walk."

He nodded, and she continued on to a scrubby bit of brush. On her way back to their wagon, Rachel noticed several men sleeping near the campfire. No one was watching her, so she detoured a little to find Patrick among them. She eased closer and could see him smile in the dim light. Resisting the urge to brush the hair from his forehead, she stepped back.

Being so close to a man she longed to kiss awake couldn't be proper at all. Rachel went back to the wagon. Her dream had been to live and work in Santa Fe. But every time she talked with Patrick, her heart wanted to follow him.

Once at the wagon, she saw Isaac was awake. A little surprising, given the early hour. "Good morning."

"Morning." He rubbed his eyes. "Have you been up long?"

"No. Long enough to take a walk."

"Mm-hmm," he mumbled while climbing down to where she stood. "Breakfast?"

She smiled, knowing what he wanted. "Yes, and coffee first."

"You're my favorite sister," he said while shuffling toward the scrubby brush along a dry creek bed.

Soon, Rachel had a full fire going, coffee simmering, and ham sizzling in the Dutch oven. Isaac approached, scratching the back of his neck. "If we were near a river, I'd ask if you fell in," she teased.

"No such luck." He sat cross-legged on the ground next to her. "Some of the men were trading war stories, and I fell into the conversation." Isaac took the cup of coffee she gave him. "I almost miss being around other soldiers."

"You're not in the army anymore, though."

He took a sip. "No, and sometimes—well, I won't say I miss it. Miss the people, though."

Rachel nodded, understanding what he meant. She missed having lady friends, especially now while in an all-male group. The gentlemen had all been mannerly, but weren't close. She dropped dough into the pan. Maybe one was, but she didn't think of Patrick as a friend.

"Good morning."

She looked up with a smile. "Good morning, Captain."

"I wanted to make sure you knew we'd be at Dodge by midafternoon. We'll likely not stop for a noon meal."

"So we'll get to see your new command?" Isaac asked. "How easy do you think the transition will be?"

"I won't know until I get there." He waved off Rachel's offer of coffee. "It's my first time to be completely in charge."

Isaac took the offered coffee for himself. "The soldiers won't take you seriously. I'd watch out for resentment from officers who feel they should be in your place."

He squatted next to her. "I have several good men in my command, so I'm optimistic about the assignment."

Rachel had difficulty not being mushy over his enthusiasm. Patrick's confidence in his plans complemented hers and contrasted Isaac's pessimism. "Do you know what sort of place it is?"

"A little. The fort is new, built over the summer. I expect the buildings will be a lot like Fort Larned's, except newer."

She smiled despite a developing sense of dismay. "Sounds wonderful. I'm excited for you." He would never leave such a plum assignment, and she couldn't blame him. After their overnight or two at his new post, Rachel would never see Patrick again.

# CHAPTER TEN

Patrick stared out over the collection of sod huts and dugouts. A swamp of liquid he didn't want to know about lay to the south. What the wind blew over left him ill. "So, this is my new command."

Lambert shifted in his saddle, the leather creaking. "I'm afraid so, sir."

No trees. No railroad to bring supplies. Trade wagons passed through and a few rolled by just now. He sighed. A new fort meant, he supposed, too new to have been truly built yet. "Very well. Let's continue on and see how much we need to accomplish."

Rows of the dug-in homes lined up along the Arkansas River's north bank. What he'd mistaken for sewage had just been the slow-flowing river. They rode up, and he let Lambert do the talking while he assessed the situation. There was to be no transfer of power because the former commander had died in the last Indian attack. He interrupted to say, "I'd like to see where injured soldiers are kept."

"We don't have a hospital yet. The wounded and ill

stay in their bunks during treatment," the active commander said.

"Which is?" Patrick asked.

"Whiskey most times, light surgery when we can manage."

"When you can manage?"

"The surgeon died from pneumonia, we think. He coughed a lot."

Somehow, the news didn't surprise him. He'd learned enough from Cahaba to know sanitation mattered. "Have you sent requisitions?"

"Yeah. We'd ask and never get enough."

He nodded. Supplies had barely reached pre-war amounts. He visually inspected every soldier within eyesight. The men stationed here were dirty, and after he dismounted to peer inside Patrick realized why. Bunks were cut into the dirt of each dugout. A fire with a hole in the top for air and light to come in regulated the temperature.

Several of the homes reeked of sickness as the soldiers lay there, too ill to move. His jaw soon ached from gritting his teeth. The dangerous conditions rivaled any he'd experienced at Cahaba.

He looked around at the men gathered. They all waited for his assessment. "The installation is unacceptable. We need an infirmary, proper waste disposal, fortifications, an armory, and a hundred other things." Patrick turned to the interim commander, a first lieutenant in a dirty uniform. "There are no officer quarters other than the dugouts?"

"No, sir."

Patrick glanced at the man. He seemed terrified. "Very well. Are there any empty quarters at all?"

"A couple. We'll have to dig a couple more for all of your men."

"I'll gather them up... Your name?"

"Harper, sir."

"I'll gather them up, Harper, so we'll have more hands working." He turned to his first officer. "You'll see they get the word?"

"Certainly."

"Let's get started as soon as the livestock are cared for." Patrick and Lambert went to the supply wagon for shovels. Harper followed, and he turned to the man. "Do you have a process for choosing where to build a house next?"

"We just move to the right or left, depending on if there's a high enough bank or not."

He exchanged a look with Lambert. "Fine. Let's find at least four and start digging. We won't be nearly done by tonight, but I'll feel better with a head start." He waited while his first officer let down their wagon's tailgate before reaching in for a shovel. "Our men will dig while yours will offload supplies. I'd prefer the sickest among you do nothing more than direct where the goods will go."

Harper turned to a soldier. "You heard?" he asked, and the other man nodded. "Carry out his orders."

"Yes, sir."

He turned to Patrick. "I'll show you the next dugout we had marked for the commander." The trio began walking. "We didn't bother after his death because we had enough housing."

"Understandable." They reached the place. A few shovelfuls had been excavated. He asked an approaching Douglas, "Is everyone on their assignments?"

"They are."

"Let's get started so we'll have someplace to live while I fill out requisition orders." He began digging, as did his first officer. After a few scoops, Harper wandered off, returned with a shovel, and joined in as well.

Soon affected by the afternoon heat, he followed his first officer's and fort's interim commander's example and unbuttoned his shirt. He lay the fabric out over the prairie grass like the other two men and continued digging. The gusts of wind, while warm, were dry and helped keep their bare skin cool.

"Excuse me?"

Patrick turned to see Rachel. "Yes, ma'am? Is something wrong?"

"No. I don't think so."

Her voice, a little breathless, matched the heavy-lidded stare she gave him. Heat warmer than any boiler room filled him. Affection, attraction, and amusement had shown on her face before now, but Patrick had never seen desire in her eyes. With a slight grin, daring her to be honest, he asked, "What do you want, then?"

"To know if you need any help. I do happen to have a shovel."

He heard a slight chuckle from Harper and frowned. Patrick wanted to clobber the guy for being disrespectful. "No. You may not help us dig under any circumstances," he growled.

The hunger in her eyes dimmed, and he scowled. She was an angel for wanting to help. Or, he wondered as she glanced up from the ground to his bare chest, maybe she was feeling a little devilish. Any sane man would welcome her attention. He wiped the sweat from his brow and wanted to see her smile. "Although, all of us would welcome you and your water jar."

She gave him a teasing grin and a tiny curtsy. "I'd be glad to bring you all a drink, Captain. I'll be right back."

Patrick watched her leave for a few seconds before getting back to work. Rachel would be the right wife for a commanding officer. She thought of others and their needs. She had known hardship and didn't mind rough conditions. Even better, she'd seen him dirty and sweaty yet still seemed to desire him. He sighed, blowing the hair up off of his forehead. The woman indeed was everything he'd ever dreamed of for a wife.

"Do you think the Stewarts will be safer on the Cimarron route or the mountain route?" Patrick asked.

"To Santa Fe?" Harper asked, and at Patrick's nod he said, "Neither. Attacks have happened all over between here and there." He stopped and planted the shovel in the ground. "They're better off waiting for a larger group to blend in with. Even then, there's no guarantee Indians won't get them." He nodded to their south as Rachel returned with their water. "I'd hate to see what they'd do to a pretty girl like her."

Patrick glared at him. "They'll do nothing because they won't dare."

"Right, sir. They won't," he said.

She held up the jar to Patrick first. "Here you are. There's plenty more, and I don't mind refilling this for you all."

He watched as she left them again. Fury filled him as the secret fantasies he'd had about moving on to Fort Union with her now evaporated in the face of reality. She'd move on to Santa Fe, yet he couldn't leave his or any other soldiers in this Godforsaken fort. Rachel disappeared behind a wagon, and his anger switched into sorrow. His throat hurt and nose stung. By the end of the week, he'd never see Rachel again.

\*\*\*

Rachel couldn't get Patrick's bare torso off her mind. She sucked the slight sting from the end of her finger. Sewing while distracted wasn't her best idea. Once word spread how she was a seamstress, every man able to get around came over with mending. A smart woman would teach them all to sew. She shook her head. Everyone had too much work to stop and learn a new skill. Maybe once real buildings were up, she'd have time...

She paused. They'd be in Santa Fe by the end of the month. No teaching and worse, no Patrick. Rachel refocused on her task. Her dream had been to live and work in New Mexico, not burrow into the dirt like prairie dogs. Not even if Patrick were here with her. Her eyes ached with tears. Love didn't happen so fast. She hardly knew him well enough to even like him.

Isaac came over and sat on the tailgate beside her. "I don't recognize that shirt."

"I'm not surprised. It's one of the soldier's. Captain Sinclair was kind enough to share their water during the *Jornada del Muerto*. I thought I might do some mending for them."

"Hmm. It's going to be difficult for you to leave him behind, isn't it?"

"Well, yes. A little."

"I thought you didn't trust him."

She didn't stop sewing and couldn't look at her

brother. "I wasn't entirely honest. He's honorable, trustworthy, and will make some woman a fine husband."

"Some, but not you?"

"We're going to Santa Fe, remember?" She straightened out the shirt and checked for any other mending needed. "Our dream is to live there on our new farm. Restart the life we should have had in Missouri."

"Funny thing about dreams is they can change."

"Not mine." She couldn't look him in the eye. "I've dreamed of being a businesswoman from Santa Fe, and that's what I'll be."

"In that case, you'll be one as soon as we're on the road tomorrow morning."

She glanced up at him, her throat tight. "Tomorrow? Seems awfully soon, doesn't it?"

Isaac stared beyond her. "What do you think, Captain? Will we be able to leave first thing in the morning?"

Rachel turned to find Patrick there, fully dressed. She had the urge to cling to him and beg him to let her stay no matter the cost. "Or should we wait for a while? Maybe help with the new homes, laundry, and other odd jobs?"

He sat beside her. "You should go. The fort isn't suitable for ladies. At least, I wouldn't want you here with us. The conditions here are worse than I expected, and I'd prefer you didn't have to endure them."

"I'm a lot tougher than I look."

"You are, I'll agree." A breeze blew stray hairs into her eyes. He brushed them away with a caress. "Except there are hostiles between here and Santa Fe. I'd prefer you would be in a fort with adequate fortifications instead of holes in the ground."

"How long will it take to get this place as functional as Larned, or even Leavenworth?" Isaac asked.

Patrick leaned forward to look at him. "My best guess is two years to be anywhere near Larned, and fifty for Leavenworth."

"Fifty?"

"I might be exaggerating."

Isaac chuckled. "Although, looking around here, you might not." He leaned back. "Have you heard word as to which is the better route—mountain or Cimarron?"

"I have. One is as dangerous as the other is at the moment. There's a regular supply train of wagons due here tomorrow morning, and it'd be best if you left with them no matter when they left."

Her heart squeezed, and she couldn't breathe for a moment. He couldn't really want her to go. She folded the shirt in her lap, focusing on the movements instead of the pain in her chest. The men talked around her, and she couldn't listen to any more. How could he let her leave so easily?

Patrick cleared his throat. "Harper mentioned Fort Union is older and more established. The buildings are adobe, but not dug into the ground like rats."

Rachel stared ahead. "Sounds a lot nicer than here."

"I agree. After I'm done here maybe Union will be my next assignment if there's nothing else closer to Santa Fe."

Isaac chuckled. "Maybe when you've dug enough bunks for the men, you'll ask to be sent back east where it's civilized. Take a steamer ship from Leavenworth to New Orleans. Travel around and see the world while you're a free man."

He smiled at Rachel before looking over at her brother. "You know the army has me now. I won't know freedom until they let me go."

"Which is why I left," Isaac said and shook his head. "I want to be my own person. See the world before I settle down."

Rachel turned to him. "What? What are you talking about? You want to live in New Mexico. On our farm. Make a new life for us."

"Sure, for a while." He stared ahead. "I've been thinking about life and what I want. Tied down to a farm sounded good after the war, but now that I've seen something other than Missouri and battlefields? I'd like to visit everything else there is out there."

Before Rachel could argue, Patrick said, "I hear you. I've had enough of being cooped up, living day to day. After the Sultana disaster, I realized life is short. I wanted to go west while I could, without a wife and children." He nodded toward the river bank where all the soldiers would sleep at night. "Be careful what you wish for, huh?"

"Yeah," Isaac said. "For every frying pan, there's a fire to jump into."

Patrick laughed. "True, and now I have something to look forward to."

"And what is that?" Rachel asked.

"Being anywhere but here, ma'am." He nudged her with his shoulder. "I might visit New Mexico once in a while to see if there are any good-looking women there."

"Ha," Isaac snorted. "If there aren't, you'll see me running back home. And speaking of home, did you know anyone who was on the Sultana?"

"I knew several men on there, and was supposed to be with them."

"I'm glad you weren't," Rachel said. Lincoln's assassination soon after the steamship's explosion took over the newspapers. All she really remembered was there were over a thousand people lost.

"Me too, ma'am." He smiled at her. "Very much." Patrick glanced away from her, toward the fort. "Looks like my first officer needs me." He stood. "It's been a pleasure, and I hope to see you both before you leave tomorrow."

Before she could reply, he walked toward the soldier. By this time tomorrow, she'd be a day's travel away from him. Rachel's eyes filled with tears and she hopped down from the tailgate to hide her crying from Isaac. She stacked the shirt with the others. The sun sank low in the west, making the sky too dim to sew by anyway.

"Has he said anything to you about his experiences in the war?"

"Not really." She glanced over at Isaac. His face was pale under his suntanned skin. "Why do you ask?"

"The only reason he'd be waiting for the Sultana is if he'd been in a Confederate prison. The disease and sleeping on the ground? This fort is his nightmare come to life."

# CHAPTER ELEVEN

Rachel's eyelids fluttered open at the noise outside her wagon. Who would be lighting fireworks in a hailstorm first thing in the morning? She rolled over and tried to go back to sleep. A bugle call she'd never heard before led her to sit up with a cry. The men outside were fighting. Dawn had broken enough for her to see an arrow stuck in their canvas top. Even worse, Isaac was gone.

She quickly lay back down and hoped the thick wooden sides stopped bullets. Gunshots boomed startlingly close sometimes and other times farther away. A scream from someone hit occasionally rang out in the morning air. The smell of gunpowder filled her nose whenever she took a breath, choking her.

Her throat burned while she lay there and tried to not hear the dying men all around her. The minutes crept past in a slow drip. The fighting went on until the shooting eased to a stop. Moans from the wounded rose in volume. Bile bubbled up in her throat, and she prayed no one lay outside gravely injured.

A man jumped onto the wagon. She screamed, startled until seeing it was Patrick who held her. Rachel relaxed against him. "Oh, thank God you're all right."

"Shh, it's over." He rocked her in his arms. "You're safe."

"What happened out there? Where's Isaac?" She pulled back and looked into his eyes, scared from the worry evident on his face. "Is he, you, everyone all right?"

"Indian attack. Short, but lethal. Rachel, your brother's been hurt, but he'll be fine. One of our medically inclined men is removing the arrow from his arm."

Rachel shared the worry in his eyes. She took in a shuddering breath before saying, "I need to see him."

"Come on." Patrick helped her down from the wagon. "I'll warn you. There'll be other wounded and some dead."

"I understand." She tried to be strong but as soon as she saw his first officer's body, she gasped. "Oh no!" She buried her face in Patrick's chest. "He's not—"

"Yes," he ground out. "One of the first."

She began sobbing. "I'm so sorry."

"So am I." He wrapped his arms around her and gave a squeeze. "Come on, darling. Isaac will want to know for sure you're safe or he'll never stop complaining."

She nodded and clung to him as they walked. "You're right. He does like to grumble about everything." Rachel recognized a couple more of the men, one wearing a shirt she'd returned to him last night after dinner with a new button. She sobbed.

He held her. "Do you want to stop for a moment to gather yourself?"

"No. Isaac needs me." She hugged him closer. "I'm glad you don't."

"Need you?" he murmured. She nodded, and he pulled away to stare into her eyes. "Darling, I will always need you. Always."

"Oh," she whispered, and tears filled her eyes. "I need you, too."

He hugged her closer, and when she looked up at him he kissed her. The world stopped around them. Her imagination couldn't have ever conjured up how perfect his lips felt against hers. Strong, hungry, and all man, she wanted every bit of him for the rest of her life.

Patrick began nuzzling his way across her cheek, stopping at her earlobe and saying, "Don't go. Please stay with me forever."

"Yes, I will. Forever." As soon as she said the words, every muscle of his tensed.

"I'm sorry, but no. It's not fair, and I shouldn't have asked. You can't promise me such a thing." Patrick held her away from him. "You have dreams. I can't ask you to give them all up for me."

"And yet I could ask you to give up yours?" She held his face in her hands. "My dreams are now yours. Living without you would be a nightmare, Patrick. I can't leave."

He didn't move for a moment before hugging her again. "My darling. I've loved you from the moment we met. Every day since has led me to dread saying goodbye to you."

"We can't leave each other…"

"No, we can't." He rubbed his thumb over her lips, smiling when she gave him a kiss. "Marry me today. Be my wife and I vow I'll make a Santa Fe woman of you in a few years."

Her lips still tingling from his touch, Rachel nodded. "Yes, I want to marry you, and will hold you to your promise."

Patrick kissed her again before saying, "Let's tell Isaac about our plans. I'm sure his fury at our news will get him on his feet in no time." His hand slid down to hers, and he led her to where her brother was being cared for.

As soon as they stepped into the circle of wagons gathered to protect the wounded, Isaac groaned. "Oh God, tell me no. You two aren't getting married."

She and Patrick looked at each other. He grinned and asked her, "Has he always been a good mind reader?"

"Sadly, yes. He's far too perceptive for my own good."

"Great," Isaac moaned. "Now I can't die in peace because you'll stay here and give me all sorts of nieces and nephews to spoil."

Rachel's face burned at his insinuation. "Well, we haven't talked so far ahead."

"I'm sure it'll happen sooner rather than, ow!" He turned to the second-lieutenant-turned-doctor. "Have a care, will you? Arrowheads hurt."

She hurried to the side opposite his injury. "Do be careful." Rachel peered at the deep scrape. "Wait, where's the arrow?"

"On the ground somewhere," he sighed. "I don't know. I didn't save it as a souvenir."

Narrowing her eyes, she glared at him. "You've had worse injuries tree climbing back home." Rachel shook her head and motioned at the medic. "Go on and tend someone who truly needs help. Do you have a needle and thread? I can easily sew him up myself."

"No, don't let her," Isaac said and looked at Patrick. "She'll make flowers and leaves all along the scar."

"Sounds pretty," Patrick replied before turning to Rachel. "Don't you need colored threads?"

She chuckled. "There's no need. I'll keep him as utilitarian as possible." After giving a glance at Isaac, she hugged Patrick and said, "I know you have plenty of other more serious tasks. We'll be fine until you're finished."

"Yes, darling." He kissed the top of her head before leaving.

As soon as he was gone, she asked, "Are you fine with our plans? He really should have asked you before proposing to me."

Her brother shrugged and winced from the pain. "Do you love him?"

"I more than love him." She settled in where the officer had been tending Isaac.

"Do you like him?" he asked with a yelp as she began sewing.

"Of course. Who wouldn't like him?"

"Remember what Ma always said."

She chuckled. "I do. Loving is easy, liking is far more difficult." Rachel tied up the end of the stitches.

"Lucky for me, Patrick is easy to like and love."

"I'm glad you found him." He stared up at the clear sky. "I only have one regret. When you marry, I'll have to live up to my big words and actually explore the world."

\*\*\*

Patrick regretted wearing his uniform jacket during the Indian summer afternoon. Still, he couldn't marry the love of his life half-dressed. He gave her a shy glance. Another wagon train had stopped in the evening, and they happened to have a group of ladies. Rachel had been thrilled to not be the only woman in the area.

Isaac stood next to Rachel with a rare smile on his face. If Patrick had to guess, he'd bet his bride's new friends lit the man's spirits. Helping-the-ladies-fever had affected all of the nearby men, it seemed.

Not him, however. He stared at the minister and tried to pay attention to the words. Patrick had already had his fill of chatter today. His mother would either be overjoyed to have a new daughter-in-law or furious she'd missed the ceremony.

He glanced at Rachel again. The women had wound little wildflowers in her hair and given her a bouquet to carry in one hand while she held his hand with the other. The ribbons tying up her glorious blonde hair were probably borrowed, too.

"Patrick, do you take Rachel Analisa Stewart to be your wife, to have and hold from this day forward?"

He took a deep breath, his heart in his throat. "I do." She squeezed his hand, and he smiled at her. As the preacher talked more, Patrick couldn't look away from her.

"Rachel, do you take Patrick Michael Anthony Sinclair to be your husband, to have and hold from this day forward?"

"I do."

"By the authority vested in me by the State of Kansas, I declare you man and wife. Captain Sinclair, you may kiss your bride."

His troops catcalled and he grinned before sweeping her in his arms. "Are you sure you want this life with me? We'll have difficulties, especially here in the middle of the wilderness."

"Yes, I'm more than certain," Rachel replied, and pulled him closer for a kiss hot enough to blaze a new trail to New Mexico and back.

# BONUS MATERIAL
## Dmitri's Heart

Continue reading for an excerpt of Dmitri's Heart, the fourth book in the American West series.

# Chapter One

"Did you meet Beth?" Samuel Granville brought Anne Galway's hand to his lips. "She's a lovely woman, albeit not as beautiful as you."

She smiled when he glanced up at her. The man was far too handsome for his own good. His tanned skin brought out his twinkling blue eyes. Every time he returned from one of his trips over the Oregon Trail, he looked a little older. The sun also brightened his usually dark hair. "Yes, I have, and you're right. Nick did well in marrying her."

He winked at her and let go of her hand. "She didn't do too shabby herself, marrying into the Granville family and all."

Anne laughed. "So I've been told." She stepped closer to him. "When do we set a date for our own marriage? You've promised this was your last trip east without me."

Sam put his hands on her shoulders to pull her into a hug. "Hmm, I'm not sure. How do you feel about a springtime wedding? Say, in May or June?"

Her heart sank, yet Anne struggled to keep a smile on her face. She marveled that he could wait until spring while Nick and new wife had married before reaching Oregon Territory. How had passion been given to one brother and not the other? She ignored her dismay and kissed his cheek with a smile. "Sounds perfect. I'll begin planning. I have plenty of time to change my mind a hundred times between now and then."

Sam chuckled. "In that case, I'm sure you'll need every minute. Just don't change your mind about me."

"Oh?" She leaned back to stare him in the eyes. Needing more of a declaration from him, Anne prodded, "So you do want to marry me?"

His eyebrows rose. "Of course I do! You're beautiful, a true Irish rose." He pulled a long corkscrew tendril that had escaped her bun and let go so it'd bounce back into place. "Right down to the hints of red in your chestnut hair. Plus, your eyes are the color of summer leaves. It's perfect we marry among the June rosebuds."

She tilted her head. His words were a good start for sure, but she hadn't heard the exact phrase vital to any marriage. "You have to love me for more than my heritage and beauty, don't you?"

Sam laughed. "Fine. You're fishing for compliments and I've been remiss in giving them." He knelt on the Persian rug and held her hand with both of his. "Apart from your appearance, your solid family and their financial acumen, which you happen to share, your charm and grace, and finally your wonderful fashion sense, I love you for how you make me laugh and needle me for yet more praises than I already give." He stood and brought her chin up. "And I love you for the long history we share. I can't imagine another woman more flawless than you. The rest of our lives together will be perfect."

"You always say the most charming things." Anne

pulled him over and sat on one of the parlor's chairs. He took a seat close to her and she smiled while searching his clear blue eyes. He'd answered appropriately, yet, had he? Still, she didn't feel as if her heart believed him. "There's no other girl you'd rather marry?"

"Certainly not." He leaned back on the poppy red settee and let go of her to put his arms behind his head. "Why would you ask? I'm charming to other women, but you're the one I want."

His lack of action nagged at her. In a perfect world, he'd insist on a Christmas wedding next month. Anne stood, anxious to pace the floor while in thought. Maybe she was too impatient and pushy. He'd never acted as if she were anything but his one and only. But, she needed him to desire her and so far, he didn't seem to any more than in a "next spring" way. "I suppose I am," she replied and turned to him. "You're always devoted to me when in town, anyway."

Sam frowned before smiling. "Oh, I see. I didn't send enough love letters to you while on my way back, did I?" He patted the seat beside him and she complied as he continued, "I'll have to spend this winter convincing you of my love and grand passion." He put his arm around her and kissed her cheek. "And help you plan the most romantic wedding the west coast has ever seen."

His answer helped sooth her neglected feelings a little more and she relaxed against him. "All right. I'll let you." She smoothed an errant lock of black hair from his forehead. "Will you be joining us tonight?"

"For what, dearest?"

The blank look on his face irritated her. "Oh come

on, Sam. The dinner party?" He could remember a thousand and one details about the expeditions he'd been on but not the events important to her? "You must know you're one of the guests of honor tonight. You and this new business partner of father's are the main reason for the event at all."

His eyes narrowed. "New partner, huh? Just to your father?"

Sam's suspicion exasperated her. One moment he acted disinterested, but the next? She shook her head. "Yes, he's some sailor who's been all over and is a valuable contact for international trade. He and a few of his people will be there. You're supposed to attend as my fiancée and future business owner. Tell me you'll be there."

He leaned back, letting his arm fall from her shoulders. "Would love to, darling, but I can't. I'm already spoken for at Nick and Beth's reception."

Anne raised an eyebrow at him. Sam had to be playing a joke. He wouldn't choose a delayed party over an important dinner with her. Especially not after his having spent most of the year with Nick and Beth already while in the wilderness. "They've been married how long?"

"I know." He leaned forward, staring her in the eyes. "You know I'd be there if I could. It's important to Mother that she launches them into polite society."

She stood, unable to keep the frost from her tone. "Fine. I'll just inform my parents of your cancellation."

Sam also stood and turned her around to take her hands. He began swinging their arms as if paying a mutual childhood game. "Come on, now, sweetest, don't be angry. I've just arrived and you have to love me."

Anne gently pulled from his grasp, still irritated yet a little more mollified due to his smile. "I do adore you. I'm just very disappointed over finding we're at cross purposes tonight."

He hugged her, giving Anne a light kiss on her nose. "Not cross purposes so much as representing our families. You'll represent me at your father's to-do and I'll be you at mother's reception."

"Ha!" She snorted before remembering her manners. "Does this mean you'll be in one of my dresses?"

After a chuckle, Sam responded, "I don't know about that shade of yellow on me, but you'd be beautiful in my trousers." He slipped out of her grasp and began backing out of the room. "Give my regrets to your family and keep Saturday open for me, all right? There's a dance I want us to attend."

"Very well. Saturday is yours." She followed him to the large foyer, both of their heels clicking on the Spanish tile floors. "You'll be at the next dinner party, promise?"

Sam opened the heavy wood door and a gust of fresh air blew inside. "Absolutely. Count on it."

Anne watched as he strolled down their walkway before she closed the main door. She leaned against the closed front door and stared up at the foyer's crystal chandelier. After a quick glance at the ornate grandfather clock chiming the hour, she shook her head. He'd been back in Oregon City for two weeks and they'd spent an hour of that time together. Only one hour.

She'd planned on spending the entire afternoon

with Sam. Her mother was overseeing the servants in the hotbox of a kitchen and didn't need her help. None of her friends would be free to call on, either. She climbed up the curved staircase, specific steps squeaking more than the others.

Once in the privacy of her bedroom, she sighed and slumped against the closed door. The very idea of listening to a night of economics and business dealings bored her to tears. Sam being with her would have kept the evening bearable. She would have to make do with any kindred person among the attendees.

Her spirit brightened. Anne never turned down the chance to make a new friend. She went over to the ornate bed and kicked off her shoes before lying down. Although, her father hadn't mentioned if wives were included in the dinner party. She assumed so.

Sam most likely had left her a seventh or ninth wheel for tonight. She groaned and rolled over onto her stomach. Her meeting and falling for a handsome new suitor would serve her reluctant fiancé' right. He needed a reminder of who she was in town.

# ABOUT THE AUTHOR

With an overactive imagination and a love for writing, Laura Stapleton decided to type out her daydreams and what if's. She currently lives in Kansas City with her husband and a few cats. When not at the computer, you'll find her in the park for a jog or at the yarn store's clearance section.

If you enjoyed this book, please consider leaving me a review. I'd love to learn more about my readers so if you prefer, you can contact me via the links below. I always welcome constructive advice and hoped you liked reading this story.

Find me online at https://twitter.com/LauraLStapleton, www.facebook.com/LLStapleton and at http://lauralstapleton.com. Subscribe to my newsletter to keep up on the latest and join my Facebook group at Laura's Favorite Readers.

Made in the USA
Las Vegas, NV
18 January 2023

65837442R10069